The Sleeping Tiger

Other Books by Marjorie McEvoy:

CALABRIAN SUMMER

ECHOES FROM THE PAST

THE QUEEN OF SPADES

EAGLESCLIFFE

WHO WALKS BY MOONLIGHT

THE WHITE CASTELLO

THE GRENFELL LEGACY

SOFTLY TREADS DANGER

NO CASTLE OF DREAMS

Marjorie McEvoy

THE SLEEPING TIGER

DOUBLEDAY & COMPANY, INC.
GARDEN CITY, NEW YORK

1983

All of the characters in this book
are fictitious, and any resemblance
to actual persons, living or dead,
is purely coincidental.

Library of Congress Cataloging in Publication Data

McEvoy, Marjorie.
The Sleeping Tiger.

(Starlight Romances)
I. Title. II. Series.
PR6063.A196S5 1983 823'.914
ISBN 0-385-18277-5
Library of Congress Catalog Card Number: 82-45362

Printed in the United States of America

First Edition

For Sara-Ann,
another brave girl

The Sleeping Tiger

CHAPTER 1

May 1857.

India had changed very little from the India Andhra dimly remembered as a little girl, back in 1842. The same atrocious unmade roads, the same oxcarts plodding slowly along, sending up clouds of choking dust, the same parched landscape, waiting breathlessly for the monsoon to break.

What tears she and Jenny had shed when forced to leave it and patient Ayah for far-off England, to be educated in a cold, alien land, with only Aunt Emma to welcome them on the holidays.

Now it was all behind them.

"They're coming!" Jenny gasped, jigging up and down in great excitement on the hard bench outside the barrack walls. "I can hear the music!"

Every neck of the officers' wives and daughters crowding the benches craned to the right, eager to catch the first glimpse of the ceremonial parade. As the native pipes and drums shrilled more bravely at the head of the procession, a great shout went up from the Indians lining the road opposite. Flags and bunting, as highly colored as the saris of the women, were waved aloft. "Salaam, salaam!" they called. "Salaam to Prince Vinita! Salaam to the Begum and the heaven-born baba."

And then as the first elephant drew near, inevitably carrying the Maharajah, another roar from the crowd. *"Ha, ha, Maha Deva!"* "Hail, hail, Lord Siva!"

Andhra gasped in admiration. She had forgotten how magnificent these parades could be. The great stately elephants, the proud mahouts astride their heads, the gorgeous trappings, the rulers in the silk-draped howdahs under golden ceremonial umbrellas, the flashing jewels and cockaded turbans. To one recently arrived from England, they were like an exotic dream.

After the ruler came his elder son, Prince Vinita, his wife, the Begum, and the new arrival, the cause of all this rejoicing, for in the course of time, the dusky baby in the arms of his ayah would in turn be the great Maharajah.

Flowers were strewn beneath the elephant's feet, the pipes shrilled more loudly, the cymbals and drums clashed in wild abandon.

"How happy the Begum looks," murmured Jenny.

Andhra's attention was elsewhere, on the third elephant, whereon rode a dark-eyed young prince who positively took away her breath. Never had she seen such proud carriage, such devastating looks, so magnificent a uniform. And with the same golden-brown skin as she herself.

"Who is he?" she gasped.

The officer's daughter sitting on her left just caught the words above the din.

"That's Prince Ranjana, the younger son," she enthused. "He's sailing for England very soon, to complete his education at Oxford. He particularly asked for an English partner at the dinner tonight, so that he could practice the language, and guess what! I'm the chosen one, as the senior unmarried daughter of the regiment."

Heaven help the Prince, Andhra reflected cynically. Here was a plain Jane if ever there was one, and no doubt that was why she remained a miss. Now if *she* herself were the chosen one . . . true, she was Indian-born, but had lived most of her life in England.

Grimacing, she reminded herself that she and Jenny were scarcely known here yet, and were lucky to be invited to the dinner and ball at all.

"There's Father! Doesn't he look splendid!" Jenny's glance was on the British contingent, when after the stately elephants the cavalry rode up on their gleaming horses, to the lively sound of the regimental band.

Andhra nodded. Her thoughts were still on Prince Ranjana

and the coming festivities. What a mercy she had brought out that daring ball gown from England. What had that saucy young seamstress at the dressmaker's said of it as she fitted it on?

"Why, miss, you look quite stunning! Mark my words, you'll be married to some handsome young officer before you can turn round, once you reach India."

A fig for some English officer, Andhra pouted. In comparison with the Prince, they receded into limbo. Her brown eyes snapped fire as she recalled the palace on the hill, as remote from the crowded streets of Chandipur as chalk from cheese.

Well, at least she would see that from the inside tonight, and also Prince Ranjana, if only from a distance.

The procession over, they made their way to their waiting carriage, to be driven back to their father's bungalow on the outskirts of the town. Most of the army bungalows were nearer the garrison, but Father had preferred to live away from his place of duty. A happy arrangement when Mama was there to make life run smoothly, but since this atrocious climate had carried her off, he must have been terribly lonely.

"How careworn Father looks at close quarters," Jenny whispered as they drove slowly along the bumpy road, past oxcarts and barefoot Indians.

"I'm glad we were able to come out here at last to be with him until the threat blows over."

Andhra's glowing face sobered under its raven hair and wide-brimmed hat. *If* it blew over. The cloud was darker than Jenny realized, or perhaps any of them. The wives at least refused to believe that anything so ghastly as a rebellion could break out anywhere in India, least of all in the little garrison town of Chandipur. Surely the Indians, Hindus, and Moslems alike, thought too highly of the British to ever turn against them, they reasoned.

"At least for today we can forget it!" she declared with a strained laugh. "'Eat, drink, and be merry, for tomorrow we die' sort of thing!"

"How can you say such a thing, tempting providence?" Jenny's delicate face, a pale shadow of her vivacious adoptive sister's, whitened visibly as they turned into the compound of their bungalow.

Waves of heat rose up at them as they stepped from the carriage. The brassy sun was at its height, showing mercy to no living thing. In spite of the efforts of the Indian boy, the garden had wilted to a parched wilderness, with only the pipal trees, under their ripe figs, thriving. It would be a relief when the monsoon came, unpleasant though that could be.

"A light lunch, then bath and rest until evening," Andhra said, already feeling the perspiration trickle between her breasts as she entered the shaded veranda.

They picked at the curry, drank cup after cup of Darjeeling tea, then made for the so-called bathroom, where Ayah waited to minister to them.

It was merely a stone-floored apartment with a drainage hole in the center and a couple of chipped hip baths. They plunged gratefully into the tepid water, then suffered Ayah to shower and towel them, Andhra with a sense of irritation because, though twenty-three, Ayah still bossed her around as she had done twenty years ago and still called her "Missy."

She was quite unconscious of the delectable picture she made standing tall and slim on the wet stone, her golden-brown skin an alluring contrast to the pallid white of sister Jenny's. For though they looked upon each other as sisters, and could not have been more devoted had a blood tie existed, they were only so by adoption.

Andhra, born of high-caste Indian parents, understood she had been orphaned at a tender age, and adopted by Major Hilton and his wife as a playmate for their only daughter. When old enough they had been sent to England together to be educated in the time-honored way. Gradually, Andhra's past had all slipped away. She became English in speech, dress, and outlook. Jenny was her sister and Major Hilton her father. Only her golden skin, her lustrous black hair, her liquid brown eyes, and her innate poise and beauty proclaimed her true origin.

Plus her spirit. She possessed the high courage and endurance of the women of her race. The unbending will that enabled them to work twice as hard as their menfolk. To give birth in the rice paddies and then finish their work without a whimper.

Ayah loved her all the more for it. All those school years she had longed for the day when her Indian missy would return, a lovely, cultured young woman.

And Andhra had quite lived up to her dreams, even though she had acquired some tomboy ways, not fitting to a young lady, in that cold gray land of England.

"Now go and take your siesta, my pearl of great price," Ayah murmured, draping a cotton robe round the golden shoulders.

Both Andhra and Jenny hated the shroud-like mosquito nets around the beds. They seemed to cut off what little air there was, but had to be suffered, to prevent the worse suffering inflicted by lurking mosquitoes.

Soon hot and sticky again, Andhra tossed and turned, but eventually dozed off into a light sleep that lasted until Ayah awakened her with more tea, the one beverage that was the salvation of the women at least.

"The Major is back," she said. "Time to get up now and dress for the ball."

"Stunning" was the right word, Andhra realized, gazing at herself in the long bedroom mirror half an hour later. The blue silk of her gown, with its elaborate ruching and frills, was exactly the color of the Indian sky, and the cutaway bodice revealed more of her firm young bosom than she had ever shown before. Above it glowed her eager face, arrestingly lovely with its brown eyes and golden skin, framed by the glossy black curls that Ayah had cunningly coaxed from her hair.

Their father, glancing in to see if they were ready, echoed a similar sentiment with a long whistle.

"I can be proud of my women tonight! At last I can be glad you're not the son I always wanted, Andy, my dear."

Andhra smiled at the old pet name, conjured by him when she had been an unruly little tomboy, scorning the dolls her sister played with and demanding soldiers and drums.

"Jenny's equally attractive!" she declared, noting her sister's wistful expression as she stood in her pale pink gown.

Quite untrue, of course, but Andhra had always shown a fiercely protective air toward her delicate little sister.

"Well, come along, girls, we mustn't be late. This is a very, very important occasion, and your first launching into local society. I'm sure you will both do me credit."

Outside, in the brief dusk, it was scarcely any cooler. Not a breath stirred in the heavy, waiting air. Waiting for what? The monsoon, or something more sinister?

In spite of the warmth Andhra shivered. Not until they were bowling along the road in the carriage could she escape from the shadow that seemed to be growing over these garrison towns in northern India.

Once Chandipur had been simply a small Indian town, with its bazaars and hovels clustering about the Rhamsing Palace, splendid on its hillock. Then the East India Company, backed by the British Crown, had entrenched itself in this strategic spot, with a river nearby for transport and miles of good level land adjoining on which to build one of those startling new inventions, a railroad. Eventually this would stretch to the great port of Calcutta, an ideal base for the tea trade and any other lucrative commodity on which they could lay their hands.

Inevitably a British garrison had followed, to keep order, protect the company's interests, and uphold the glory of the renowned Queen Victoria.

But it was toward the old quarter they now drove, slowing to a crawl as they nosed into the crowded alleys leading up to the palace. Aghast, by the light of the carriage lamps Andhra caught glimpses of pitiful bundles of rags that were actually people huddled by the roadside, the only home they knew. She had forgotten how cruel this land could be to the untouchables.

A greater contrast to the Rhamsing Palace could scarcely be imagined. All tinted marble, graceful arches, and soaring cupolas, surrounded by gardens that had, in spite of the climate, kept their freshness. Here, carriages were arriving, shedding their loads, and departing. Lights blazed from the palace, bursts of music floated out, and all was bustle and animation.

Prince Vinita and the Begum, backed by the Maharajah, greeted them in the great marble hall, perfumed with flowers and incense. As they turned away, Colonel Rawlings, chief of the regiment, bluff and bearded, strode up.

"Ah, there you are, Hilton! Glad to make the acquaintance of your charming daughters. I've a request to make to Miss Andhra. A request from the Maharanee, so it's more a command," he said, touching their hands.

Andhra's brown eyes widened. She was all attention.

"Miss Blenkinsop, who was to have partnered Prince Ranjana at dinner, unfortunately went down with an attack of migraine at the last moment. As the Prince is on the point of leaving for Oxford, he particularly wishes to have the latest news from England from one recently there. Also to practice his English. You should fill the bill admirably, Miss Andhra, being so English yet of his own race."

"Why, thank you, Colonel. I'll do my best." Her heart beat faster. How marvelous of fate to step in and grant her secret longings in such a fashion. Poor Miss Blenkinsop. Too much excitement, or sun.

"That's settled then. Now you can circulate until dinner is announced."

Andhra passed the intervening time in a dream. The Indian ladies were like exotic butterflies in their brightly colored saris, she reflected, and yet, tonight, the Prince preferred an English girl. Was he promised in marriage to some unknown, highborn Indian, as was the custom in this country? It was more than probable.

The Colonel's lady enlightened her on the subject when she paused for a chat a little later.

"How fortunate that you're able to step in for Miss Blenkinsop," she gushed. "And you've no need to stand in awe of the Prince. He's informal and easy to talk to. He should have been married by now, but the girl chosen for him by his parents died of the smallpox quite recently, so he's off to college until other arrangements can be made. Now you must excuse me, my dear."

So presently Andhra found herself seated at a sumptuous table, all shining silver and flowers, illuminated by the soft light of candles in great, golden candelabra. On one hand was a gawky young Englishman from the East India Company, and on the other, Prince Ranjana.

So close, he was even more devastating than at a distance. His scarlet turban flashed with jewels, his native dress fell in luxurious folds about him, caught round his supple waist was a cummerbund of cloth of gold. Even these elaborate trappings distracted not a jot from his masculinity. He was as magnificently virile as a Bengal tiger.

Briefly she told him how she had been adopted by the kindly major and his wife when she had been too young to recall her past life.

"So now you can enjoy the best of both worlds," he said, smiling, "and how beautifully you carry it off, if you will pardon my presumption."

Eager, high-spirited Andhra soon found herself as much at ease with him as though she had known him all her life, talking of London, the English scene, and the new railroad that was beginning to revolutionize travel, to his great delight.

"They are building it here," he said. "The people are uneasy. Scared of progress. They prefer the more traditional oxcart or riverboat, but who asks their opinion? Tell me, Miss Hilton, what do you think of India, now that you've come back to it with new perceptions?"

The dreadful poverty was the most striking thing, she admitted frankly. Such a stark contrast to the ruling class. "Why don't you do something about it, or do you never take a close look at the starving wretches cluttering the streets to the very fringe of your palace? Now I expect I've offended you, but you did ask," she ended.

He shrugged his slim shoulders. "You are uncomplimentary, but I prefer frankness to criticism behind one's back. I can only say it is the custom, but that is no valid excuse. My father and brother take it for granted, but when I return from Oxford, I shall try to improve matters, for I confess that I, too, am not happy when I ride out and see the extent of it. Because it has always been with us is no reason to believe that nothing can be done."

Her brown eyes filled with admiration. "How splendid to hear even one voice raised in the face of apathy. I do wish you luck in your efforts!"

"If the day ever dawns when I can begin on such a daunting task, Miss Hilton," he said somberly.

"Now you must explain that enigmatic remark."

He sighed. "A darkening cloud is spreading over this part of India," he continued. "It threatens us all, but most of all the British. Have you not heard whispers? No, of course, you have only recently come out. I have no desire to alarm you, but I greatly fear the sleeping tiger is stirring, and who knows where it will end if he roars into wakefulness and pounces to destroy?"

Andhra's lips grew taut. "There are indeed rumors, and my father seems worried, but I don't understand much about it. Tell me, Prince, what is this threat?"

He said reluctantly, "There is trouble with Indian infantry in a few outflung places. They are the scapegoats and the instruments of rebellion, but the real culprits are the deposed rulers. In some cases they consider the British have treated them unfairly, and are inciting the troops to turn on the infidels who filched their estates and are now their masters. It is an explosive and fearful situation."

"But surely only isolated," Andhra said stoutly. "Here in Chandipur, for instance, relations between the British, the Indian troops, and the rulers like your family have always been excellent, I believe."

"That is so, Miss Hilton, but who knows what may happen if the trouble spreads? However, this is no place or time to speak of such dismal possibilities. We are supposed to be rejoicing, and truly I could not wish for a more bewitching dinner partner. Come, drink a toast with me to our further better acquaintance, for I don't intend to stay in Oxford indefinitely."

Brown eyes gazed into brown, and something warm and

deep passed between them as they sipped their toasts, nonalcoholic in comformity to his religion. Andhra's years in England seemed to slip away, leaving only two vital young people of this burning land poised on the brink of discovering each other.

He leaned toward her so that no one else might overhear.

"I wish I could dance all evening with you, but alas my card has been filled with duty dances. They have left only one for my dinner partner. It is number thirteen. You will keep that one for me, Miss Hilton?"

She nodded, already imagining the delight to come, his hand enclosing her own, his supple form in contact with hers.

Although she had no lack of partners, including dashing young Captain John Ravenswood, one of Father's officers, who danced with her three times, she could scarcely wait for the thirteenth number. Then, instead of leading her out onto the crowded floor, the Prince drew her through a doorway, along a corridor, and out into the extensive garden at the back of the palace.

"I've had enough of dancing," he said, laughing. "It is much nicer out here, just the two of us alone."

How she agreed. In the pale moonlight, the flowers looked ghostly, the shrubs cast strange shadows, and down a flight of steps a fountain splashed into a silvery lake.

He drew her toward it, her hand in his as though they were carefree children.

"I'll remember this evening, and the lovely Miss Andhra, when I'm far away in your cold England," he murmured. "Say you'll remember me."

"Always." How could she forget the first man who had ever touched her heart? A man of her own race and a prince among men.

The charged beauty was almost palpable. A thousand perfumes stole out from the unseen blooms. Above glowed the stars, pale and remote. The moon, hanging big and low, was like a heavenly lantern. No sound broke the magical silence beyond the occasional rustle of a nocturnal animal and the sound of night insects.

The golden moments could not last. As if to emphasize that time was running out, from beyond the towering wall enclosing the garden, where the creeping jungle began, came a sound both startling and shattering. The roar of a tiger on the prowl.

"A potential man-eater," the Prince said, frowning. "A hunt will have to be organized. How I wish I could be here to take part."

The tiger wakes, Andhra thought, unable to suppress a shudder, shattering the harmony of the night. And more prophetically, of northern India?

As though the same trend of thought flashed through his mind too, he dug into some hidden pocket and brought out a tiny soft-leather pouch.

"You may be in great danger," he murmured, "while I am safe in England. Take this amulet, and wear it always about you. The princely god Siva will protect you. His power is great."

She drew back. "How generous of you to be so concerned for me, but in England it is unconventional to take gifts from men we have only recently met."

He made an impatient gesture. "But this is India, and you are an Indian maiden. Time means nothing. I feel that we met not today but many moons ago. You feel the same. I know it."

She nodded. It was undeniable.

"Then take it, wear it, and think of me when you look at it." He thrust it into her hand.

Unable to resist him, she dropped the tiny pouch, warm from his body, into the beaded evening reticule that hung from her arm. How disapproving Jenny would be when she saw it. Jenny was so conventional, while she herself secretly chafed against such irksome rules.

Before she could say any more, a staccato explosion broke in on them, shattering the peace of the garden.

"Listen, the firework display is beginning at the front of the palace," he exclaimed. "They are too good to miss. Can you run, dear Miss Andhra?"

"Try me!" She hitched up her graceful skirt, grasped the

hand held out to her, and together they raced along the path toward the palace. Here he turned off on a driveway skirting the building as being the fastest to the forecourt.

They never reached it, for dashing past a side gate, standing wide, they were almost knocked down by a horseman galloping in as though all the hounds of hell were on his trail.

The Prince held up an imperious hand.

"Halt!" he ordered. "The palace is celebrating. Surely you know? What is so urgent that you storm the place like this?"

The horseman drew rein and leaped to the ground, bowing low to the Prince, whom he evidently recognized.

"Grave news, Your Highness," he gasped. "It is rumored in the spice bazaar that disaster has overtaken Meerut. That the sepoys have mutinied and massacred their officers, that the city shall fall under fire and pillage, and that few of the white usurpers or their families shall survive."

Andhra froze in horror. This was too much and too sudden, in spite of the earlier rumors.

The Prince, too, looked stricken. "So it has begun already," he muttered. "Time has run out. The tiger wakes, and who knows where or when his lust to kill will cease?"

She moved at last like a sleepwalker startled from a beautiful dream. "I must go and warn Father," she whispered, turning her back on him with an air of finality. Her golden dream had ended while scarcely begun, and with it, had she known, the golden era of British India.

CHAPTER 2

It had all started at the very beginning of that fateful year, 1857, with Aunt Emma's death. Andhra and Jenny had remained in England with her after the completion of their education to care for her during her last frail months. The months had stretched into two years, and Andhra had raged against fate whenever she thought of her father, now alone and needing her help and companionship, out in faraway India.

With Aunt Emma's passing came relief. The house was put into the solicitor's hands, the trunks packed, and at last here they were, sailing down the Ganges River with Major Hilton himself.

"It's good to see you, Andy," he had said when he met them in Calcutta, reverting to her childish nickname. "It's been lonely since my poor Elinore was taken, I'll admit."

"You need taking care of," she scolded, noting his careworn expression. "I believe you've been neglecting yourself, or else you've some nagging worries. Well, now I'm here you can tell me."

He smiled briefly. "You always had the courage of a boy. I'll admit I'm glad of it now. I must say, this is not exactly the moment I'd have chosen for your arrival here. Two months back all seemed well, but events have moved swiftly since then, unfortunately."

Andhra frowned in perplexity. "Then everything is *not* going smoothly. You haven't picked up malaria or something, have you?"

He shook his head. "It's nothing personal, my dear. Just the way things seem to be going with the Indian troops. There's nothing in Chandipur one can lay one's finger on. It's mainly atmospheric. The attitude of the sepoys is changing. They're less keen to please and more prone to shirk duties. That, coupled with rumors, is worrying."

His glance was on Jenny as he finished. He might have been more explicit with Andhra, but clearly he did not want to upset his younger daughter. Jenny had always been delicate and highly strung. Andhra had shielded her from childhood up, shouldering her burdens with loving solicitude. Now she changed the subject, waiting until her sister's attention was on the passing river scenery before she looked expectantly at her father.

"If there's anything I ought to know, you can tell me now," she said quietly. "I promise not to panic."

He was silent for a moment, then unexpectedly he asked. "How would you like to learn to shoot?"

She stared. "The thought has never entered my head. Young ladies don't go in for that sort of thing in England. However, you know how keen I've always been on outdoor activity, Father. If you think it necessary, I guess I'd soon learn."

Inwardly, a small cold fear feathered her spine. Things must be graver than he admitted for him to even consider the notion.

"I should feel more at ease if I knew you were capable of defending yourself, your sister, and the bungalow while I'm away all day at the barracks," he admitted. "For the first time, I'm beginning to regret its isolation and wishing it were nearer other officers' families."

Andhra dimly remembered the long carriage drives to and from the town. Two British women alone among hostile Indians would be in a vulnerable position indeed, but she had never been one to panic.

"As I remember our Indian servants, they'd protect us to the death," she said with a pretense at lightness. "However, if it will make you less worried, I'll gladly learn to shoot. I guess there's nothing to it for a tomboy like me."

"Good girl! Oh, Andy, you really ought to have been a boy." He laughed, but his eyes were moist.

"We'll start as soon as we reach home."

He shook his head.

"That could be too late. Much better to start now. You know what long stops these riverboats frequently make to collect wood for fuel, besides merchandise and food. It happens to be the custom for sporting males to make short forages into the jungle in search of peafowl, quail, or other fresh food, rejoining the boat before it sails. It should cause little comment if I take you with me."

She laughed. "It sounds exciting. I'll tell Jenny, but not the reason behind it."

Andhra joined her sister at the rail, their pet dog Patch at her heels. It had seemed too much of a wrench to leave him behind in England, so they had brought him along. Father had been quite glad to see him. "He'll be some measure of protection, small though he is," he had said.

Jenny smiled when she heard the news, considering it just another of her sister's tomboy pranks. "At least Patch will welcome the breaks ashore," she declared. "You can take him along."

So it caused no comment whenever the boat stopped for a while and Major Hilton, the dog, and Andhra scrambled ashore. Clad in safari suits and boots, they would wander along among the tangled growth, never penetrating more than a few yards from the river for fear of meeting a tiger or a deadly snake.

Patch was a great help in flushing the birds. The Major unerringly shot those fit for the pot, and in between showed her how to carry and hold the gun, and later load it.

Jenny would stare in mock horror when they stepped aboard again, disheveled and muddy. The very sight of a gun filled her with alarm, yet Andhra experienced a strange elation, especially after she was permitted to try a shot herself, and actually winged a duck at close quarters.

Father's enthusiastic "Well done, Andy!" amply repaid any discomfort of sticky heat and insects, invariably experienced as soon as the jungle closed about them. She was almost sorry when the arrival at Kangarh put an end to further progress, for here they were to leave the river behind.

It would have been thrilling to stay awhile and explore the

ancient city, but Major Hilton's leave was almost up and he was anxious to rejoin the regiment. So the girls caught only a glimpse of the crowded bathing ghats, the beggars, and the rituals, and then packed themselves and their baggage into the carriage that Nayan, the groom, had brought to meet them.

The overland journey of three days was less pleasant. Clouds of dust rose to plague them from the unsurfaced road, dry and rutted from the long drought. The countryside around wilted visibly, gasping for the monsoon as yet far off. The searing breath of the hot season now made itself felt, and even Andhra was glad to slump on the carriage seat, wiping the perspiration from her brow and fanning herself with a banana leaf.

"As soon as we're settled in I'm leaving off these tiresome stays!" she declared. "The Indian women have the right idea, with their light loose draperies and bare midriffs. We should follow suit."

"You'd run into opposition!" Father laughed. "The army wives are sticklers for convention, even importing heavy Victorian furniture from England. It creates an illusion of home, I suppose."

"Then thank goodness we shan't be living in their midst," she said, laughing.

The nights of the journey were spent in Dak bungalows, primitive enough, but supplying rough beds, a meal of rice and chapaties, and fodder and rest for the horses. On the rough road they passed groups of Indians going about their daily work, in bullock carts, on the occasional camel, on foot, or perhaps on a working elephant, which afforded some diversion, but they were all glad to arrive, dusty and weary, at the bungalow Andhra dimly remembered. In its parched compound, it stood so isolated and peaceful that her father's earlier unease seemed quite unfounded. What *could* go wrong here, with the British so entrenched, respected by Hindus and Moslems alike?

It was almost sundown.

"Just time for you two girls to have a tub before dinner," Major Hilton suggested.

But they had to renew acquaintance with the outside before going in. They rushed excitedly round the compound, recalling childish days. It seemed to have shrunk in their absence.

"A real pair of madcaps you've brought out from England," called an amused voice from the open gateway.

Andhra stopped in her tracks to stare at the newcomer. A big, tough-looking fellow, with face burned almost as dark as an Indian's by outdoor life. A great contrast to Father, for instead of a smart uniform, his clothes were casual to the point of untidiness, and his unruly red hair was devoid of covering.

"Glad to see you, Copeland," Father called back from the veranda. "Come and meet them. After being cooped up traveling for weeks, they're full of high spirits, so make allowances."

Feeling at a distinct disadvantage, Andhra went to meet him, followed by Jenny.

"Girls, this is Mark Copeland, engineer in charge of the new branch-line railroad the East India Company are laying down. They plan to build a big locomotive depot, so he'll be around for a long time. A pukka sahib, and an old friend of mine, so you're likely to see a good deal of him. Mark, meet Andhra and Jenny, with a great deal to learn about this country, so perhaps you'll help teach them."

The newcomer smiled. "Most women bore me, but as your two are scarcely more than fillies, I'm willing to overlook their sex and do what I can."

"Fillies indeed!" Andhra exploded. "Why, I can outride most men and shoot too, even though I never handled a gun before this trip, so don't imagine I'm one of your simpering misses, angling for compliments."

"Andhra!" remonstrated Jenny, but Mark Copeland did not seem to care. Suddenly he was deadly serious as he turned to the Major.

"So you've taught her to shoot, Hilton. Very wise of you. Most of the British still persist in burying their heads in the sand, in spite of the growing unrest."

Again Andhra felt a touch of fear, dispelled as soon as they entered the spacious living room of the bungalow, for there stood Ashoka, the head bearer, deferential and welcoming, and beside him old Ayah, incredibly wrinkled now, who had stayed on all these years. She embraced them warmly and ordered the boy to bring warm water to the bathroom, then shooed the girls before her to the primitive place.

"I feel a distinct aversion to Mr. Copeland," Andhra said as they splashed around in the confined tubs. "One of the supercilious males, I fear."

Jenny, to her amazement, flew to his defense. "He was only being frank, after all. His eyes were very kind and honest, or didn't you notice?"

This was so out of character, coming from shy Jenny, that Andhra could only stare. "He's evidently the kind one likes or loathes instantly with no shades in between," she ended flatly.

"Well, don't settle for loathing yet," Jenny counseled. "If the situation is as tricky as they seem to think, we may yet be glad of a trusty friend."

Her sister nodded. "I suppose you're right." It was a relief that young Jenny seemed to be taking the threat so calmly.

He was still there when they emerged, fresher and cooler, onto the veranda. He and the Major looked sober, as though they had been discussing weighty topics, but cast off gravity when the girls appeared. He stayed to dinner as a matter of course, and Jenny seemed pleased, but closer acquaintance did not dent Andhra's hostility. The girls he obviously regarded with amused tolerance.

"He's a true-blue Britisher," Major Hilton declared when he had gone. "The right sort to have around in any emergency. He's doing a good job on the railroad and getting the best out of none too cooperative Indians. Unfortunately, they're too hidebound by tradition and religion to foresee the benefits it will bring in quicker transport of goods and materials. What was good enough for their ancestors is good enough for them. That's the way their minds work."

They'll never change, Andhra was thinking, when her father broke in: "To turn to more frivolous topics. You two are both invited to a dinner and ball at the Rhamsing Palace next week.

I found the invitation among letters waiting for me. The Maharajah is celebrating the birth of his first grandson, who will eventually succeed him. It's bound to be a glittering affair, so I guess you'll both enjoy it. A good opportunity to meet the regimental officers and their wives too, as they'll all be there."

Jenny looked apprehensive. Meeting a strange man in her own home was one thing. Being plunged into a chattering throng of strangers quite another.

"Don't be a goose," Andhra chided when she said as much. "Remember the new ball gowns we've brought out. This will be just the chance to show them off. We must put on a good front for Father's sake."

"Well said, Andy. The Indians love pomp, so spend money like water on these occasions, even though the British have annexed half their possessions and wealth. Perhaps the day will come when we wish we'd treated them better. Oh well, call me when the tea arrives. I've some work to do in the meantime."

Darjeeling tea was a great favorite with the British in this enervating climate. The ladies had it served in the late evenings, though the men usually preferred a chotapeg. Ashoka brought in the tray around ten o'clock, along with a plate of tiny rice cakes. How regal he looked in his snowy robe and turban, Andhra thought as he set the things on the round table and asked if she needed anything further.

His manner was respectful enough, yet Andhra did not fail to notice the strange expression on his face. It seemed to mask an odd sort of pity.

Unpacking occupied the following morning. After tiffin, with the Major on duty, the long hot afternoon stretched before them. Having not yet acquired the siesta habit, the girls debated the best way of filling it.

"Why not a drive?" Andhra suggested. "Our parasols will keep the sun off us and the old city should be interesting."

The carriage ordered, Nayan tardily brought it round from the stables and servants' quarters at the back of the bungalow. He seemed reluctant to drive them to the bazaars, when asked to, with the evasion that they would be closed during this hottest part of the day, and suggested a short drive out into the country instead.

"No, we wish to see the old town again," Andhra persisted, childish memories of exciting excursions in charge of Ayah dimly at the back of her mind. "Especially the Rhamsing Palace."

Still reluctant, he settled them in the carriage and drove slowly off, leaving a trail of dust in their wake.

Presently they reached the crossroad that led to the army barracks and fort. Here stood a sentry box, normally manned by one or two sepoys. Andhra still remembered how important she had felt in the old days when, as they drove past in charge of Ayah, the sentry had smartly saluted the missy babas in the Major's gleaming carriage.

Now Nayan glanced almost apprehensively at the red-painted box. It was quite empty.

"Strange," she murmured. "There ought to be someone on duty."

They drove on, to the great gateway in a crumbling high wall enclosing the old city. Here Nayan halted, again clearly unwilling to enter.

"Old city hot and dusty at this time of year, missy baba," he said. "Very dirty. Not good place to go."

"Nevertheless, we are going. Drive through, please."

"I don't think you should have insisted," Jenny murmured uneasily. "Things don't seem to be the same as they used to be."

The dirt and stench were the same, at any rate, and the heat and flies. They buzzed around the patient oxen, pulling lumbering carts through the garbage-strewn streets, and settled on the chapaties and sticky sweetmeats displayed for sale outside dark little shops. Flimsy shanties of cardboard and rusting tin crowded between these shops, and in front of all sprawled sleeping humanity, stretched out in filthy rags among garbage and the droppings of the sacred Brahman bulls.

The few people who remained awake peered at them with

lackluster eyes, or mouthed words which perhaps fortunately they could not understand. Until they reached a sadhu, a bearded holy man with long hair and strangely painted face, squatting by the roadside like some hideous god. As the carriage rolled slowly by, he lifted his grubby fist and shook it menacingly, his expression quite malevolent.

That was really sobering. Andhra immediately ordered Nayan to turn for home. They had seen enough.

The following days passed without incident. Major Hilton spent long hours at the garrison, and always looked grim and anxious on his return. When questioned he answered evasively. The girls would have seen no visitors had it not been for Mark Copeland, who rode over from the railhead twice in the late afternoons, on the plea that he wanted to make sure they were all right.

Perhaps that was all, though Andhra teased Jenny unmercifully.

"The rough diamond has really fallen for you!" She laughed. "That proves I don't outshine you too much."

But when the evening of the ball arrived, and Ayah had helped her into her new gown of blue silk, all ruched and ruffled, the long mirror reflected a magnetic woman of grace and beauty, with lustrous black curls and eyes that were like deep brown velvet.

The rebellious tomboy duckling had at last emerged a swan.

And at last she was glad to be a woman, for that one shattering glimpse of Prince Ranjana riding by in the procession that morning had revealed half-formed longings as yet quite unknown to her. Longings that both delighted and shocked her.

The Cinderella evening more than lived up to expectations, with fate casting her as the Prince's dinner partner, and the magical moments in the garden. It could have ended as wonderfully, but for the horseman riding through the gates like a fury with his warning of disaster at not so far-off Meerut.

As Andhra turned away from the Prince, whispering that she must warn Father, he caught her by the arm.

"Take care, or panic will result," he warned. "The celebrations are nearly over. Let them finish before the news is broken. It would be considered a sign of very bad luck for the new heir if the rejoicing were cut short by such tidings."

Andhra paused, biting her lip. "I've no wish to spoil the party, but I can't act as though everything were normal. The British officers have a right to know if what they feared is already breaking out. I must at least tell Father and leave the issue to him. He's far too diplomatic to do anything likely to cause panic."

The Prince nodded. "I understand." And then in a more somber tone: "Dear, dear Miss Andhra, I greatly fear for you. Who knows where the tide, once unleashed, may end? Whom it will sweep away and destroy? I beg you to wear the amulet constantly, and let princely Siva Rama protect you. He is greater than the most powerful of men."

She nodded, suddenly conscious of his hand still clasping her arm, of his dark eyes gazing down at her, warm with something more than admiration. Something she had never before seen in a man's eyes. God in heaven, she thought in a rush of feeling, why show me paradise, to immediately snatch away the cup? Why, why?

"Who knows, we may never meet again," he was murmuring in a voice almost breaking. "But while life remains, I shall remember you always, the bright and beautiful star that crossed my heaven. An Asian pearl, in spite of your British association."

Bending, he pressed his lips upon hers, gently at first, and then with a passion undreamed of. For a moment she was swept away on a magic carpet of strange and burning desire, as his arms enfolded her and crushed her against him, as though to protect her from all the horrors he envisaged.

Then, while her senses were still reeling, he released her and melted away into the scented night.

As though in a dream, emotionally battered first by the devastating news and then by a vision of ecstasy such as she never knew existed, Andhra stumbled round to the forecourt of the palace to where the fireworks were being let off.

Where was Father? She must find him.

Presently she came upon him watching the display with young Captain Ravenswood, who had shown such an interest in her earlier during the dancing. Her chaotic emotions must have shown clearly, for Major Hilton took one glance at her and asked sharply, "What's the matter? Are you all right, my dear?"

Briefly, she passed on the shattering news brought by the horseman. "I happened to be cooling off in the garden with the Prince at the time, and promised him not to cause a panic by blurting out the news to the entire assembly," she added.

"Of course. We can pray it's merely a bazaar rumor, but I fear that's just wishful thinking," he said on a sort of groan. "Thank the Lord the fireworks are ending. There goes the set piece, so we can make our excuses and leave without comment. But first I must put the Colonel in the picture. What a blow it will be to him, poor fellow!"

"Find your sister and make your way to our carriage," he called as he started off. "Ravenswood, you might take care of them. Andhra looks quite shaken."

She was certainly glad to presently find herself seated in the carriage beside Jenny, who, knowing nothing of the new threat, looked serenely starry-eyed after a good deal of Mark Copeland's company. It seemed cruel to cloud her evening, but she could not long be shielded if the news was true, so while waiting for their father to appear, Andhra mentioned the rumored rebellion in Meerut, emphasizing that it was as yet unconfirmed. Before she had finished, the Major arrived and they drove off.

"If anything drastic has happened the news will surely have come through to the garrison on the new telegraph wires," he said, then gave orders to Nayan to drive there before going home.

There was no comfort to be had there. A state of suspense and speculation reigned among the men on duty, for Meerut had gone off the air completely.

"The lines have obviously been cut, which looks grim," Major Hilton said somberly when he rejoined the girls in the carriage. "All we can do now is prepare for the worst. Pray heaven the trouble won't spread this far, but we must be ready with our plans if it does. At least we've had some warning, unlike the poor devils at Meerut."

Neither of the girls slept much. It could have been a magical night, both of them having encountered for the first time a deep awareness of the opposite sex. But starry-eyed dreams were overshadowed by stark reality, and the anxiety of wondering what the coming days held in store.

One glance at their father when they met for breakfast showed that he had not slept either. His worry was obviously at having to go off on duty and leave them for many hours in the isolation of their bungalow.

"Normally, the wives, children, and ayahs would have left for Simla or other hill stations by this time," he said, mopping his brow, "and would not have returned until the end of the rainy season. This year it was postponed out of deference to the Maharajah and the coming celebrations. I fervently wish you two were safely in the hills, but I doubt if anyone will think of going now, with this uncertainty hanging over us. It's a long trek, and under the circumstances there could be ambushes."

"If trouble really is coming, I don't suppose any of the wives would want to desert their husbands," Andhra reflected. "I'm sure Jenny and I couldn't bear the thought of leaving you alone to face it, having only just joined you."

He smiled ruefully. "That's the worrying thing. You've not been out long enough to have made friends and have people call, and this bungalow is so isolated. Even so, I doubt if it would have achieved anything. The women are going to be wary of driving around the countryside without protection now, I fear."

"Don't worry so much, Father," Andhra said crisply. "I can handle a gun now, remember, and I shan't hesitate to use one on any renegade who tries to harm us or our property. Remember, we have Patch to warn us of any stranger's approach, and help scare them off."

The Major pressed her shoulder. "Brave Andy! I'm proud of you."

"There's one friend who calls," Jenny broke in. "Mr. Copeland makes a point of coming over frequently on one pretext or another."

"Good old Mark! I'd forgotten him. I couldn't think of anyone I'd rather have around in case of trouble," the Major said, his expression lightening a little.

It was dashed almost immediately, for as they rose from the table, Ayah pattered in to wish her missies goodbye.

"But where are you going?" they asked in surprise.

It transpired that word had just reached her of the serious illness of her daughter. The woman had not long to live and wanted to see her mother above all things.

"It is not too far off," Ayah said. "I shall travel by bullock cart, and when all is over, I shall return."

It was just one more straw in the wind of change that seemed to be rising against them. Sadly the girls embraced her, wishing her a safe journey and a swift return, but Andhra felt a cold touch of fear when she gazed into the rheumy old eyes. For there, quite clearly, she saw the stark truth. Ayah knew all about the threatened holocaust and was mortally afraid for them. Her muttered words were a benediction on them, for it was written in her stars that she would never again see her missies.

Major Hilton broke the strained silence when she had left the room.

"Trials never come singly, unfortunately! Now I must go. There'll be a lot to do at headquarters. One thing you must promise me, girls. Be sure and stay within the compound while I'm away. Our servants are loyal, thank the Lord."

"But for how long?" seemed to hang on the air as they promised and watched him stride from the room. Silently, they each wondered how they were to get through the long, sultry day that stretched interminably before them.

CHAPTER 3

Even during late morning the compound became unbearable. The sultry heat pressed down on them like a stifling blanket. Overhead, the sun shone brassily, and their wide-brimmed hats did little to ward off its intensity.

"We must go in," Jenny said, wiping her clammy palms on her equally clammy handkerchief, "or we'll end up with frightful headaches."

There was nothing really to keep them outside. Everything looked dispirited, dusty, and wilting. Exactly as they themselves felt, Andhra reflected.

They had reached the veranda when a burst of barking from Patch alerted them to the intruder. She glanced sharply toward the gate, but was reassured by the sight of a bent old Catholic priest, in rusty black and wide-brimmed hat.

"Pardon my intrusion," he said as he reached them. "I heard the Major's daughters had recently arrived from England and felt a little anxious about you, knowing your father was forced to spend long hours away on duty."

"How kind of you," Andhra said. "Won't you come in and take coffee or tea with us? I was just about to order some."

"Thank you, my dear. It will be welcome. One almost longs for the monsoon in this atmosphere, trying though that can be."

"Have you walked far?" Jenny asked in concern when he was seated on the shady veranda.

"Not too far. Our bungalow is the nearest one to yours actually, but scarcely noticeable from the road, behind the pipal trees. We are two retired Catholic priests who stayed on here until it was too late to bother returning to Ireland. I'm Father

McTavert, by the way. We were happy enough until lately, but now things are beginning to look grim."

She nodded. "It is rumored that trouble has already broken out in Meerut, but Father couldn't get any definite news last night, as the wires had apparently been cut. It's very alarming, especially for elderly folk like you."

He shrugged.

"Oh, it doesn't matter so much about us. We've lived our lives, my child. It is young girls like you two who are most vulnerable. One shudders to think what might happen."

He broke off abruptly, as though anxious not to scare them too much, and then the coffee came, to create a diversion.

Afterward, he said a brief prayer, sprinkled them with holy water, and took his leave, remarking that he was glad they at least had a dog to give warning of any stranger's approach.

The afternoon dragged. They tried to rest in their bedroom, then rushed out to meet him when Patch barked a welcome to the Major.

"Any definite news?" Andhra urged, not encouraged by his set face.

"Without doubt there's real trouble in Meerut," he said heavily. "Apparently the local bazaar is alive with lurid rumors, but owing to the severed communications, we can't get any concrete details through. The entire garrison is in a state of tension."

Just before dinner, they were surprised when Mark Copeland walked in on them without the formality of knocking. The Major took one look at his tired, grim face and thrust him into a chair.

"Things must be bad to send you out here at this hour," he said.

Mark Copeland nodded. "I rode hell for leather to warn you as soon as news filtered through from a railway source. It appears that three regiments of the Bengal Indian infantry at Meerut ran amok, shot their British officers, battered down the gates of the jail, and let out the prisoners. Joined by this mob, they rushed through the cantonment looting and burning the bungalows, and massacring the women and children, leaving the place a shambles. Now it is feared they are making for Delhi."

Even the Major looked too stunned for words. At last he said, almost groaning, "So now there's no doubt whatever that there's treachery in the ranks. Where will it end? God help us all."

Jenny, stunned with shock, sank into a chair and began to cry softly. Violence of any sort had always terrified her.

Andhra clenched her hands. "What in heaven's name started all this?" she demanded. "The British used to be as revered as minor gods. It seems unbelievable."

"Not really," her father said heavily. "Some of the British authority became too high-handed. Several of the Indian rulers have been complaining for years of their lands being annexed without due payment, and their power whittled away. There have been minor disturbances before, but nothing on this scale. They are the instigators, no doubt."

"And the final spark was those new Enfield rifles," Mark elaborated. "Isn't that so, Major?"

The latter nodded and for the benefit of the girls explained. "This has been building ever since they were introduced. You see, my dears, the cartridges of these have to be greased before insertion, and the sepoys are convinced we are using animal fat for this job. It's not true, but once started, there's no ending these rumors."

Andhra bit her lip. With the pig an abomination to Moslems, and cows sacred to Hindus, they would conclude their religion was being insulted and flouted by these white infidels, and nothing was more calculated to make them see red.

Mark joined them for dinner, to Jenny's satisfaction. Her tears had ceased, but she looked the essence of frail girlhood, calculated to bring out every protective instinct in a he-man like Copeland, and he showed himself more than willing to supply his protection. It was with obvious reluctance that he refused his host's offer to stay the night.

"Sorry, but I must get back to my outpost," he said. "Now the balloon has gone up, who can tell whether or not it will affect Indian civilians? I don't know how far I can rely on my track-laying gangs. They could well go on the rampage and wreck everything if they think they can get away with it, especially as they've never been convinced of the necessity of such a mode of transport. I doubt if there's much I could do to stop them, but I'd have a damn good try."

Jenny showed dewy-eyed hero worship when she bid him good night. She was clearly well on the way to losing her heart, Andhra reflected wryly.

"Take care," he called as he mounted his horse. "I'll look in again as soon as I can get away."

There was a long silence, which no one seemed to know how to break, after his departure. Finally, Major Hilton said heavily, "Thank God you learned to shoot, Andy, though you need more practice. It will be my only comfort when I'm away on duty."

In anticipation of a dawn rise, and setting off for headquarters much earlier than usual, he went off to bed immediately, with a further warning to venture no farther than their own compound on the following day. Left to their own devices for the rest of the evening, the girls felt too restless to settle to anything.

It was then that Andhra remembered the Prince, and his amulet, warm against her breast, on a silver chain round her neck. She had instinctively hidden it without even mentioning the incident to Jenny. Now she considered the time ripe.

"We've never believed in amulets and such devices as Indians do," she said, "but if it's any comfort to you, I have something here that Prince Ranjana believes will protect us. A tiny replica of their powerful god Rama, or Siva."

She brought it to light, coloring faintly as she recalled his unexpected farewell. The burning kiss that had seared into her innermost being, awakening responses that both thrilled and dismayed her. For not only was he a prince of this land where rank counted for so much, but now there was this creeping menace to further heighten the barrier between them. She was now a member of a British family. Tragically soon they could be in opposite camps, his family aligned with the Indian troops against the usurping British, even though her blood was as true Hindu as his.

Jenny was staring in wonder at the small object with its jeweled eyes and golden form.

"Why, it's beautiful, and must be quite valuable," she gasped, "but somehow it seems rather primitive to me to believe in such superstition, whatever you think. And whatever would Father or anyone say to your taking it in the first place from a man you scarcely know?"

Andhra's color deepened, but this time it was more in vexation.

"I don't really care what anyone thinks!" she declared. "But I shall keep it hidden for fear of its being stolen. It doesn't make me less British in outlook to tolerate the belief of my ancestors."

Her sister's glance switched to the telltale face with its rosy flush.

"Andy, I do believe you're in love!" Her voice was a murmur of astonishment. Andy, the high-spirited tomboy, hitherto scornful of anything sweet and sentimental, to fall at first meeting and to one so impossibly beyond her.

Andhra unconsciously echoed the Prince's words.

"What does time matter? You yourself seem decidedly sweet on Mark Copeland on very short acquaintance. Deny it if you can!"

Jenny smiled. "Touché! So we each have a secret. Something to help us through dangers ahead perhaps." She hugged her sister, and they drifted out onto the dim veranda, too strung up to sit indoors.

Suddenly Andhra raised her head, sniffing like a terrier.

"Can you smell smoke?"

"Now you come to mention it, yes."

They descended the steps and walked round to the back of the bungalow, gazing out over the compound. At the far end was a high wattle enclosure, shutting off the servants' quarters and the kitchen where the food was prepared. By tradition, the white memsahibs never penetrated beyond this fence, but respected the privacy of the servants and their families. Now the girls were perturbed to see a glow rising from within the enclosure.

"It can't be their cooking," Andhra murmured. "Charcoal and dung braziers don't make such a glow."

"Listen," Jenny whispered back. "I can hear voices."

There was indeed the sound of voices, some of them raised in emotion. Neither of the girls could understand the language except for one word. The word "Meerut" fell on their ears like a knell of doom.

"They are talking of the mutiny." For the life of her, Andhra could not keep the quiver from her voice. "But what on earth is that glow? I wish we could see what was going on."

"The landing window!" Jenny exclaimed.

It was the only one that overlooked the servants' quarters, small and grimy, serving only to light the way to a storage attic under the eaves. Together they hurried back to the bungalow and mounted the wooden steps leading up from a rear passage.

Impatiently Andhra scrubbed at the dusty little panes with her handkerchief, ruining it forever.

"Open it. You'll see and hear better," Jenny urged.

With difficulty Andhra forced the rusty catch and pushed it wide, then thrust her head through the aperture.

"They've actually lit a bonfire!" she hissed.

With accidental conflagration an ever-present danger in these tinder-dry pre-monsoon months, to court disaster by lighting a fire in such a confined space was unheard of. Clearly something momentous was afoot.

"The servants, you mean?"

"Those, and others. They're sitting cross-legged round it, talking and gesticulating."

"I wonder who the others are."

"Probably Father McTavert's servants, his bungalow being the nearest."

"If only we could grasp what they are saying!"

"Only that one significant name." Andhra drew in her head and closed the window. "They may be simply discussing the rebellion at Meerut, or else . . ."

She trailed off, unwilling to contemplate the hideous possibility of their own servants turning on them.

"Lighting a fire points to recklessness," Jenny said soberly. "They don't fear our anger or punishment any longer. Should we tell Father, do you think?"

"Not until morning. He has enough on his mind, poor dear. We can only hope the kindness he has always shown to the servants has earned their loyalty."

They descended the steps. Jenny tiptoed to the Major's room, to make sure he was still sleeping, while Andhra moved to the living room.

Before she could seat herself she was startled by a tap on the glass of the window that looked out onto the veranda. Moving close, she peered through to see the white-shrouded figure of a tall man, hooded so that only a glimpse of a dusky face confronted her.

Her first reaction was one of shock. Here was an assailant and her gun not within reach. But before she could scream, he whipped back the white draperies to disclose, unbelievably, the magnificent dress and lithe form of Prince Ranjana.

With a stifled exclamation, she sped to the door, wrenched it open, and was enveloped in his arms as though it were the most natural thing in the world.

"My dear Miss Andhra," he murmured, his lips roving her cheek before finding her lips and silencing all speech with a kiss that sent her soaring to the moon, big and beautiful above them.

Dear Lord, if the moment could only stretch to eternity, shutting out forever the foreboding creeping ever nearer. The need for courage and coolness to face what was coming, and be strong for Jenny's sake, when all she craved for now was to forget everything, even chastity, and just be the woman newly revealed to her. The woman who would gladly give all without counting the cost.

The moonlight glinting on the blood-red ruby in his splendid turban reminded her of the fire in the native quarters, and the deceit they could be plotting out there.

"Why have you come?" she whispered. "Isn't it dangerous for you to be seen here?"

"So I disguise myself. The danger is much greater for you, my beloved. Terrible things are happening to British women and children. I cannot bear the thought of them happening to you. Come back to the palace with me, you and your sister, I beg you. I am sure the Major will agree, for he knows the dangers better than you. You can take shelter in the women's quarters of the palace with my younger sister. You should be safe from any attack there. Take me to the Major before I am seen. I would speak with him, for even your Indian blood will not save you, now that you are part of a British family."

She drew back, appalled at such a step. How could she and Jenny ever feel at home in that great sumptuous place, or desert Father in his hour of need, even should he approve of such a move.

"I can't do that," she said breathlessly. "He is taking a much-needed rest before going on duty again."

"You do not trust me, I think." He was all imperial prince now, regal, inflexible, and displeased.

"Oh, Ranjana, that's not true." She touched his furrowed brow with gentle fingertips. "But surely you understand how I feel. I'd despise myself if I deserted my father just when he needs me. Whatever lies ahead, we must face it together. The women of the regiment must stand firmly behind their menfolk. That's the way of the British at least. In danger we are always united. You see how British in outlook I am now."

He sighed. "You are right, my brave one, but if the situation deteriorates and you change your mind, a welcome will await you at the palace. In that case you must come secretly and in disguise, or the mob may turn on the palace if they believe we are plotting against them with the British officers. That would be very bad for the members of my family."

"Of course. I could never bring myself to put them in danger through shielding me," Andhra declared, "but, oh, how I appreciate your kind thought, my Prince."

"By the same logic, I dare not come here again. It may be

goodbye forever, my dear one, even though I shall not now be leaving for Oxford, at least while this danger lasts."

The finality of his tone was like a sharp pain in her heart.

"I pray not, to all the gods of the universe," she whispered huskily, touching the outline of the amulet beneath her dress.

"May the Lord Rama protect you," he murmured, "and all you love."

"And you, dear Prince."

A last lingering kiss, and then he pulled the enveloping white robe closely about him and melted away into the sultry night. The night that had become a menace.

CHAPTER 4

She stood there for what seemed a long time before she could bring herself to go inside, trying to calm her fast-beating heart and appear normal before Jenny.

When at last she did join her sister, Jenny looked at her with shocked disapproval.

"Everyone seems to have gone crazy," she said stiltedly. "Even our tea has not appeared as usual. I suppose the wretched bearer is out there at the bonfire and won't bother to make any."

At this, Andhra emerged from her nightmare.

"Oh, Jenny, how can you be such a goose!" she chided. "Our whole world tumbling about our ears and all you can think of is tea!"

The younger girl's lip trembled. "It isn't really that. It's your behavior that's upsetting me. I'd never have believed you could so stoop to a secret assignment, and with one so far above you in station too. You can't pretend you were out there alone. I glanced out when I found the room empty and saw you in the arms of Prince Ranjana! Whatever would Father say!"

Andhra controlled her anger.

"Look, Jenny, it's not in the least like that. The brief encounter was no assignment but as much a surprise to me as to you. Hearing of the atrocities at Meerut, the Prince was deeply concerned for us both. He exposed himself to ill will by stealing out here in disguise to beg us to take refuge in the women's quarters of the palace with his sister. He wanted to speak to Father about it, but I told him it wouldn't work, and in any case we could never desert Father."

Jenny swallowed. "I'm sorry, truly. I should have known

better. Can you forgive me? You'll have quite enough to bear if you've really fallen in love with someone so exalted, at this of all times." She touched her sister's hand in contrition.

Andhra smiled bleakly. "Apology accepted, and you're quite right about the difficulties. Prince Ranjana himself is staunchly on the side of the British, as is the Maharajah at present, but who knows what may happen if the situation worsens? You are luckier, thank heaven. You and Mark are admirably suited and in the same social class. There doesn't seem to be a single obstacle to snarl things up for you. Mark Copeland has everything on his side to please Father, and nothing against him."

It was decided to say nothing of the incident to the Major, but to rise early and tell him what they had seen in the servants' compound. That, certainly, he ought to know.

He looked disturbed when his daughters joined him the following morning and gave a graphic account of the incident.

"It's natural they should discuss the mutiny at Meerut," he reasoned, "but lighting that bonfire and having other servants sit around and talk with them gives it a more sinister aspect. I do wish I could slip back for tiffin with you, but that's impossible at present, with such momentous issues to be thrashed out. It's bound to be five o'clock before I can get away, so we'd better decide on a plan of campaign for you. You're daughters of the regiment, so must show courage and resource in the face of danger. First I think I'd better show you where the guns and ammunition are kept. Come, girls."

He led the way to his study, a room with which they were unfamiliar. It was a typical man's room, with rifles, pistols, and swords arranged on the walls, along with the heads of tigers and other big-game trophies.

"In the present explosive situation, this could be asking for trouble," he said grimly as he set about taking down all the weapons, stacking them in a cupboard, and then locking it securely.

"The small arms and ammunition are in this smaller cupboard," he explained, unlocking and opening it. "Shot, slugs, powder, canisters, and so forth. I want you to be able to lay your hands on them instantly if the time ever comes for you to defend yourselves."

Jenny looked scared, and more scared still when he said, "You may be too nervous to learn to shoot straight, my dear, but at least you must learn how to load various types of weapons. That could be a vital help to Andhra if your lives are ever threatened."

Jenny did not burst into tears, as once she might have done. To Andhra's amazement she gulped and said, "I'll do anything you think necessary, Father. It's quite time I grew up."

"That's my girl! I can't spare much time this morning, so we'll use caps, I think. They will make very little noise."

"Why not the real thing?" Andhra asked.

"We are not practicing shooting at the moment. The servants would hear and gossip. At all costs we must not give the impression that we're afraid of them. Come, we'll go into the box room."

He collected caps and weapons and led the way.

The box room had once been used by Ayah, when they were small and the bungalow was full. Now there were only a few trunks and boxes under their dust.

"Now, Jenny!" He placed the pistol in her hands. She controlled her repugnance with an effort, to her sister's satisfaction.

"Pull up the cock, my dear. Look, this is it. Now place a cap on the nipple, like so."

Fumbling, Jenny obeyed.

"Now pull the trigger, first pointing the gun at that old moth-eaten stag head over there."

His cool, commanding order calmed her into obedience. She complied, and gasped in surprise when it went off with a snap and a harmless puff of smoke.

"Bravo!" Andhra encouraged. "You'll be as proficient as Father soon."

He laughed. "Nothing to it, is there? Keep practicing your loading, Jenny, while I'm away, until you can do it automatically. Andy must familiarize you with the rifle too. It's a pity you can't have some real practice out of doors, but that would be unwise."

"Keep both the pistol and the rifle out of sight, but easy to lay hands on," he reminded them before going off to his long day's duty.

They felt terribly alone when he had gone. Jenny practiced loading both weapons and taking aim too, until she grew weary and they went to sit on the veranda.

In the late morning Nayan sought them out to ask if the missies would be taking a drive today and what time they wished him to bring the carriage round.

"We shan't go out today," Andhra told him. "It's so hot and the dust is bound to be trying."

His smile was somehow insolent, in a way that was quite foreign to him.

"The missies are wise not to leave bungalow, I think. Perhaps they have heard the stories whispered in the bazaar. Terrible things have happened in Meerut. No foreigner is safe. It is even said that the mutiny will spread far and wide, and Chandipur shall not escape."

"Then the rumors are false," Andhra said with as much conviction as she could muster. "Chandipur is in no danger. Our sepoys are loyal and would repel an attack if the mutineers came here. Our servants, too, are loyal. Isn't that so, Nayan?"

He would not answer or meet her glance. He merely spread his hands in a gesture of resignation and turned away without dismissal.

"Straws in the wind!" she said grimly when he had retreated. "They suggest that even our own servants may not be as trustworthy as we hoped if it comes to the point. How right Father is to insist on us doing all we can for our safety."

They neither of them ate much at tiffin. The heat and suspense robbed them of any appetite. And when the food was cleared away, they were left wondering how to fill the long afternoon that stretched before them.

So it was with the greatest pleasure that the sound of hooves ringing on the iron-hard drive sent them out onto the veranda, to see Mark Copeland dismounting and tethering his horse to the gate, in the shade of a dusty palm tree.

"How lovely to see you, Mr. Copeland," Jenny called. "We were just feeling lonely and bored."

"It's certainly good of you to call again so soon," Andhra augmented as he strode up. "We're so grateful, but you must not inconvenience yourself in this heat, and with all your responsibilities. Do sit down and cool off, and I'll get you a long drink presently."

He slumped into a chair, and now she noticed his somber expression and the haggard eyes that looked as though they had scarcely closed last night.

"You are having trouble with the track layers?" she asked apprehensively.

He nodded. "Their hearts have never really been in the job. The idea of iron monsters rushing over the land on rails breathing smoke and fire smacks more of devilry and witchcraft than progress to them. It only needed a fuse to set them off on the path of insubordination, and that has been supplied by the rebellion in Meerut. Insolence is growing, and even refusal to carry out orders. A little while longer and who knows where it may lead? Pillage of the stores and desertion, if nothing worse. I asked the Company to send out extra help, but they say that in the present explosive situation they need every man they have to guard offices and warehouses full of goods. The half-finished railway must take its chance."

"How frightful!" Jenny's apprehension for him was clear. "And you the only white man on the site."

"Don't fret for me, Miss Jenny. I can take care of myself. It's you two I'm worried about. That's what sent me hell for leather out here, not to inflict my own particular troubles on you. The latest report on the mutiny is that it is spreading. I wish your father were here, so that I could talk to him, but I don't suppose he'll be back before his usual time."

"I doubt it."

"Too late for me. I daren't leave the gang unsupervised that long."

Andhra squared her pretty shoulders. "In his absence, I'm the man of the house, by name of Andy. You can talk to me. I shan't swoon on you, or do anything else that Victorian ladies are noted for."

His smile of approval was gone in a moment as he said quietly, "Communications between my railhead and the Company in Calcutta are still intact, but I can't say for how long. The latest report was grim. Mutiny has broken out in Indore and other centers considered staunch to the British Crown. The details were so sickening that they hardly bear thinking about, let alone passing on to young girls fresh out from home. It seems too much of a risk for you to be alone here all day, so isolated."

"The two Catholic priests are not far off," Jenny said when she could speak for shock. "One of them came over yesterday. Like you, he was worried about us."

Mark Copeland shrugged. "Kind old fellows, but useless in a crisis. They couldn't put up the slightest resistance."

"But I can!" Andhra declared. "And even Jenny has been practicing loading. We're not quite so helpless as you think."

"Nevertheless, I still believe you ought to move in with some other army family nearer to the regiment," he persisted. "Promise you'll let your father know the gravity of the situation, and I'm sure he'll feel impelled to make other arrangements for you."

They promised, and while Jenny went in search of a cold drink for him, Andhra asked with concern, "And what of you, Mr. Copeland? What will you do if the whole gang turns on you?"

He shrugged. "My damnedest! I'd stake my life on the loyalty of at least a few, but if the odds are too heavily stacked against me, I'll make for the fort."

After quenching his thirst, he bid them goodbye, with an especially soft glance for Jenny, and a murmured "Take care of yourself, my dear."

"When shall we see you again, I wonder?" she called as he mounted his horse. She was as clearly worried by his danger as he was by hers.

"Who can say? Take care of yourselves, and God be with you."

They watched as he galloped off in a cloud of dust, then stood silent, tongue-tied by apprehension and the fear of saying anything that might make the other feel worse.

"If only there was something we could do!" Andhra spat out fiercely at last. "Inactivity is one of our worst burdens. Cooped up here like prisoners, not daring to stir outside the compound. No doubt the other regimental families are under the same constraint, or some of them would have been out to call on us before this."

Jenny nodded. "Poor Andhra, you always hated restraint. If it will help at all we can take a turn round the compound, now the sun is less fierce."

They donned their shady hats and called to Patch, both of them subconsciously thinking of Ayah. She would never have approved of afternoon strolls. A cool, darkened room and a siesta was the correct way for missy babas and memsahibs to spend the most sultry hours.

Would they ever see her again?

As they strolled round the dusty paths, baked as hard as concrete, the heat came up at them in a wave. The atmosphere about them shimmered in a sultry haze, drenching them in perspiration before they had gone very far.

Sadly they glanced at the small lawns, now withered, brown patches, and at what had once been flower beds.

"The garden boy has soon taken advantage of the situation and ceased watering, now that he considers we are too preoccupied to care, or too afraid to admonish him," Andhra said in dull anger. "There's little left to tempt us out, apart from the exercise."

When that palled, they wandered back to the veranda and sat, trying to interest themselves in books, until Durga, the wife of Nayan, glided up. She was young and sweet-faced, and as pretty as a picture in her graceful sari. But now her serene expression was troubled and her dark eyes wide with fear.

"What is it, Durga?" Jenny asked sharply.

"Oh, missy," she wailed, "big trouble! The bazaar is buzzing with it. The sepoys have mutinied at Habrah!"

"Habrah? So near! Only twelve miles off. Are you sure about it, Durga? Where did you hear it? You have been to the bazaar?" Andhra urged.

Durga shook her head, wringing her expressive hands in consternation. "Nayan it was who go to bazaar. There he hear terrible things about Habrah. Oh, missy, such terrible things! It is said the sepoys make big bonfire and on it burn many British. It is said that none escaped."

Andhra felt suddenly sick. It was only by a great effort of will that she kept a measure of composure and clasped Jenny's trembling hand to give her sister strength. Her voice died within her, but she found it at last and leaned toward the Indian woman.

"Durga, you at least are our friend. You are troubled to see your people turn on us, are you not? You would help us if you could, I am sure."

The Indian woman nodded. "Missies kind. They send good medicine for my baba when he is sick last week. Major also good to us and treat us well. I do not like what is happening, but what can a woman do to stop men on the rampage? They are like sleeping tigers who wake ravenous for the kill. Do not trust anyone, missies. Not anyone!"

She stopped short, as though conscious of having said too much, and with a scared glance round to see that she was unobserved, swiftly sped away.

Their faces pale, the two girls stood clasped together. Only days ago all had seemed sane and normal in this small isolated world. They had played with Durga's chubby brown baby when he toddled into their compound, gone driving where and when they pleased, trusted the servants and Indian troops implicitly. Now everything had changed to creeping horror. As in a nightmare, they longed to escape, but there was no way out.

Slowly, Andhra fought down the numbing terror and tried to recall the Major's words. They were daughters of the regiment and must show courage and resource in the face of danger.

"Courage and resource," she murmured, and then on a more positive note: "The guns, Jenny! The pistol and rifle that Father gave us. We ought to have them handy and fully loaded. Come, we'll do it now!"

With something positive in mind, they hurried to the study, took the key to the smaller cupboard from the hiding place that the Major had pointed out, and extracted what they needed.

Back in the living room, Jenny watched closely while her sister loaded both weapons.

"Now we have instant protection," the latter said with satisfaction.

"You should have been a boy, Andy," Jenny said with a shaky smile, "but I'm glad you're not. We would never have been such close companions."

"I, too, am at last glad to be a woman," Andhra admitted, fervently, recalling those ecstatic emotions that had gripped her in Prince Ranjana's embrace. "It has its compensations. Now you hold the pistol a moment just to get the feel of it."

"But it's loaded!"

"Loaded but not cocked. Look, hold it like this, then it can't go off accidentally."

Satisfied that Jenny would not fail her in a crisis, Andhra placed the weapons on the table. The mere sight of them boosted her morale. They then stepped onto the veranda again to watch for the Major's return.

Built on a gently sloping hillside, the veranda of the bungalow commanded a brief view of the dusty road, and a more distant one of the ornamental towers of the fort, about two miles off. Built centuries before by the Moguls, it had been a splendid shell when the British annexed it, reinforcing and adding to it to make a comprehensive center for the regiment. Here were the administrative block where the Major and other officers conducted the daily business, the barracks for the ranks, the ammunition stores, and everything else necessary to carry out the duties of the garrison. Being able to glimpse even a bird's-eye view of the impregnable-looking stronghold was some comfort, Andhra reflected.

Closer to home, she could just make out the sentry box at the side of the winding road. Were the two sentries on duty in normal fashion?

She breathed a sigh of relief as her keen glance caught sight of their khaki-clad forms marching to and fro, like animated toy soldiers.

"The sepoys are on duty today, so still loyal," she remarked, refraining from adding, "but for how long?"

"The nights are going to be a trial," Jenny said fearfully. "Every rustle, every night sound will scare us to death if we happen to be lying awake. However shall we stand it?"

"Let's not cross our bridges before we must," Andhra urged. "At least we have Father with us during darkness. He'll be back soon, so no scared faces to add to his burdens. Agreed?"

Jenny nodded. She really was trying her best to grow up.

And presently there he was, striding in at the gate, as upright and firm as though twenty years younger.

His expression told a different story when he reached them. "The mutiny is spreading like wildfire," he said heavily, making for the privacy of the living room.

"You mean Indore? Mr. Copeland came over and told us. He's very concerned about us and wanted to talk to you. Soon after he'd gone came the more appalling news of Habrah. You've heard of the atrocities there?" Jenny paused, breathless.

"My God, yes! Word got through via one of our liaison officers. Where did you hear it? Surely you haven't been out?"

"We know when to obey orders," Andhra said stoutly. "Apparently Nayan took French leave and the bazaar was agog with it. On his return, Durga stole across to warn us. She was most upset, poor thing. She implied that we'd better not trust even our own servants."

"That could be so." He wrenched off his pith helmet and mopped his brow, then, as his glance fell on the weapons, he asked sharply, "What's this?"

"I thought it prudent to have them loaded and ready, just in case."

His somber face creased into the semblance of a smile.

"Thank God for your resource, my girl."

"Father," she said urgently, "we've a right to know. Are *our* sepoys absolutely trustworthy?"

He hesitated, glancing from one to the other, then said slowly, "I can't be sure. There's nothing one can call open insubordination, but morale has plummeted. Several fellow officers agree with me that a close watch ought to be kept on them, but Colonel Rawlings is naïvely trusting. He insists his sepoys will remain loyal whatever happens elsewhere. It's a potentially dangerous situation."

She tried not to show her dismay. "Mr. Copeland seemed to think Jenny and I should move in with some army family living nearer the fort. Are there any other outlying families?"

"Yes, unfortunately. The McQueens live even farther out. Major McQueen is the regimental surgeon, you know, and they have three young children. He's damnably worried about them, so we called a special meeting and came up with a plan."

They looked expectantly at him.

"In preparation for this plan, should it become necessary for us to implement it," he went on, "we're a hive of activity at present. All day we've been ordering and bringing in stocks of food. Rice, tea, and lentils, such basic things, also as many charpoys as we can round up, together with bedding rolls and blankets. We're trying to make the fort a vast storehouse, my dears."

"You mean, if the worst comes we shall all take refuge there, Father?"

"Such is the intention. And as none of us can predict when the situation will be deemed grave enough to warrant such a step, we had to think up a way of summoning everyone, night or day, in a manner nobody could miss. Fortunately we have the perfect answer there in the fort."

They waited breathlessly.

"The big cannon!" he said dramatically. "If mutiny seems

imminent here in Chandipur, the order will be given to fire it twice in succession. Day or night, it makes no difference, that will be the signal to flock to the fort as quickly as possible."

As if to emphasize his instructions, he clapped his hands smartly together twice, adding, "Hesitate for no reason whatever if you hear that sound, girls. Your lives may depend on prompt action."

Though they were taut with nervous expectancy, the announcement of dinner by Ashoka put an end to discussion while they were in danger of being overheard.

Andhra surveyed the chicken curry and baked mango without interest, feeling that she would never again be really hungry. But the Major, perhaps realizing better than they what lay ahead, took a generous helping and passed the dishes.

"Eat what you can, girls. That's an order."

They were all glad when, the meal over, the dishes were removed and they could return to the topic uppermost in all their minds.

"So if the signal comes while you are on duty, I immediately order the carriage and we drive to the fort?" Andhra said as though there had been no interruption.

"Indeed! Impress on Nayan the need for haste. Imagine my anxiety until I see you both safely inside, my dears. As for Copeland's suggestion, I daresay I could arrange for you both to stay with some army family, if you would agree to it, for the time being."

"Emphatically not!" they declared. "We'll stick together, whatever happens. You've been alone long enough."

Jenny glanced pensively round the room that since their advent looked homely and lived in, with the little feminine touches it had lacked before.

"How awful to have to leave all our belongings behind! Who knows what might happen to them? But of course we may bring Patch?"

Hearing his name, the dog sidled round them, licking their hands.

"Of course, my dear. And there's no reason why you shouldn't bring a few clothes and toilet things along, providing you have them ready to pick up at a moment's notice. Indeed, it would be foolish not to, considering that we could be holed up in the fort for a considerable time. Should our servants remain loyal, they might help by bringing things out to us, but of course there's no guarantee of that, or whether they'd be allowed access."

Andhra said. "How practical of you to think of it, Father, while Jenny and I are still witless with shock. We'll see to it first thing tomorrow. Towels too. They're so necessary in this climate, and some shirts for you."

"Splendid. Now that's settled. I'll lie down and rest for two or three hours. If I drop off to sleep, be sure and wake me when Ashoka brings the evening tea."

Andhra glanced sharply at him. "You mean to sit up all night, Father?"

"I consider it wise," he said quietly. "We're so isolated and vulnerable in the darkness."

She paled, but only said, "Patch will keep watch with you. He's good company and always warns of approaching strangers."

He rose and pushed back his damp hair. "Don't hesitate to call me if anything alarms you, and don't forget, I've given orders to be called around ten o'clock."

Everything seemed abnormally quiet when he had gone to his room. They missed the pleasant evening conversation, and Jenny's session at the battered upright piano, playing favorite songs from England. They had no heart for such things tonight. How many more nights would there be here?

With the brief tropical dusk already fading into darkness, it was their turn to keep watch, they decided, making themselves as comfortable as they could in the cane long chairs on the veranda. The loaded pistol by her side, and Patch crouching between them, gave a measure of Dutch courage, and Andhra felt prepared for anything.

"Poor Patch! He knows something's wrong. He's the picture of dejection," Jenny sighed, adding, "I'm glad Mr. Copeland said he would make for the fort if real trouble threatened him too. We'll have one good friend there."

Andhra was silent, her hand going instinctively to her breast. Beneath the cotton of her gown she could feel the hardness of the gold amulet resting there, and wished with a fierce hunger that it was Prince Ranjana's dark head against her nakedness instead of his gift.

The strength of feeling appalled her. How could it have grown in so short a time, and for a man she might never see again?

If trouble broke in Chandipur, what would happen at the palace? Would the might of the Maharajah keep him and his family safe, or would the fact that he was an open friend of the regiment count against him?

Who could say? It was all part of the tension that was building up to unbearable intensity.

Jenny, dreaming romantic dreams of Mark Copeland perhaps, actually nodded off in the darkness, leaving Andhra to her thoughts. It was almost a relief when the brooding silence was broken by the croaking of bullfrogs and the cries of night birds, in the familiar pattern of night life here. They, at least, were normal.

Then the waning moon rose, to lighten the landscape a little.

Time dragged. Andhra was beginning to wonder if Ashoka had already deserted them and tea would not be forthcoming this night, when she heard the welcome sound of china clinking from the room behind.

She rose, stretched, and touched her sister's face.

"Time to go in, Jenny. Time to call Father. I wonder if he managed to snatch any sleep."

CHAPTER 5

The two girls, followed by the dog, sought the Major's room and crept in at the half-open door. The moonlight disclosed him lying on his back sound asleep. He had thrown himself down fully dressed except for boots, tunic, and belt. On the bedside chair lay his sword, along with his double-barreled gun.

"Poor Father! He looks so peaceful it seems cruel to waken him," Jenny whispered, "but I suppose we must obey orders."

Low as her voice was, it roused him. With a soldier's alertness, he started up and leaped to his feet, his hand reaching automatically for his gun.

"Gently, Father, it's only us. We came to tell you that tea is in, as we promised," Andhra said.

"All well?" He let out a mighty yawn.

"Quiet as the grave." Immediately she regretted the ghoulish metaphor, covering it with a hasty "We hated having to disturb you. You looked in need of more rest."

"You did quite right. Never disobey orders in a crisis, Andy. They could be vital."

"Tea will be doubly welcome to us all tonight," Jenny said. "What should we do in this climate without it?"

"You might go and pour it, then. I'll be out in a moment." He reached for his tunic.

Ashoka had turned up the lamp in the living room. With the tea things laid out in its beam, it presented as peaceful a picture as one could imagine. It seemed impossible to believe that dire calamity threatened them.

How they had always enjoyed these closing moments of the day, when, relaxed and healthily tired, they sat in the soft light, in silent companionship. Now, if only by the Major's tousled hair and bleary eyes, they could not pretend that nothing had changed.

"What ages away that ball at the Rhamsing Palace seems," Andhra sighed, setting down her cup. "I wonder whose side the Maharajah will be on if mutiny breaks out here."

"He's a just man, and has always been on excellent terms with the British, unlike some of the rulers," the Major said. "I'm certain he'll deplore it if the sepoys turn on us, but whatever his feelings, he won't be able to do very much against a frenzied mob. Once the Indians cast restraint to the wind, they revert to primitives and there's no holding them."

They finished their refreshing Darjeeling tea in silence, but none of them could force down any of the tempting little confections Ashoka had brought in with it. Would they ever enjoy them again? Andhra wondered.

Patch's wet nose nuzzling her hand brought a wry smile. Though puzzled by the clouded atmosphere he could not understand, he at least was ready for his usual tidbit. She passed him a rice cake and patted his head when his tail wagged in appreciation.

"I suggest coffee might be better tomorrow evening," the Major said. "A cup of strong black coffee should help to keep me awake. That is, if all goes well," he added tersely.

The alternative was too ghastly to contemplate. Was this a nightmare, or stark reality they were living through?

The same thought crossed her father's mind, for he glanced from one to the other of his daughters and beads of perspiration broke out on his brow.

"Father," Andhra exclaimed, "you can't go on long keeping watch all night and working hard at the fort all day on two or three hours' sleep. Let Jenny and me do a longer stint. After all, we could rest during the day, with Patch on guard."

He shook his head. "Not tonight, my dear, though it's brave of you to offer."

"Why not tonight?"

"Well"—he hesitated, then went on—"as I passed the sentry box on the way home, instead of saluting me as usual, the sentries looked sullenly away."

"The sentries refused to salute you, a British officer!" Jenny exclaimed.

He nodded. "You see now, girls, how explosive the situation is, and how necessary that we all be on guard at all times, especially during the hours of darkness."

"It's certainly bad when it creeps so close," Andhra murmured. Quite incredible from men who had revered the British Crown for years, had fought for them against vicious attacks in fierce hill campaigns, and had given their lives for the new White Raj. The tiger had been roused from sleep, and was stalking the land in search of blood.

Jenny looked as though she was on the verge of tears, in spite of her obvious effort at control. What would calm her and all three of them? Andhra wondered desperately.

"Jenny," she burst out, "why not play something before you and I turn in? It would be cheering for Father and make things seem more normal."

"Yes," the Major urged. "Play 'Home, Sweet Home,' my dear. It is one of my favorites."

Jenny sat down on the shabby piano stool. It cost her an effort to lift the lid and strike a few tentative notes, but presently the familiar melody stole out, and the Major began to hum in his deep bass voice. Andhra tried to join in with the words, but when she reached the closing, "There's no place like home," her voice broke and trailed off, and the piano notes petered out without the final chords.

Their father cleared his throat and bid them good night. They crept away, afraid of upsetting him before his long vigil.

For the first time in her life Andhra glanced under the bed before enveloping herself in the mosquito net. She had also placed the pistol close to hand, loaded and ready, and murmured her nightly prayer. Then, with Patch and the Major on guard, she was able to let care slip away and fall into an uneasy sleep.

At five o'clock, when the sun began its morning rout of the mists, she sprang out of bed and hastily washed and dressed.

The Major, looking drawn and disreputable with hair awry

and smart red tunic hanging loose, came in from the veranda as she entered the living room.

"I wonder if you can get Cook to rustle up some breakfast while I wash and make myself respectable, my dear," he said.

She nodded. "You look as though you've had a rough night. You really must let Jenny and me do a longer spell of duty tonight."

"Perhaps."

Neither Ashoka nor any of the boys had put in an appearance yet, so there was no alternative but to seek them out in their own quarters.

It was blessedly cool when she stepped outside. These early hours, while mist still hung around, were the only bearable ones at this time of year, she reflected as she walked through the compound.

The gate to the servants' quarters stood open. Glancing through, Andhra saw several of the wives busy with cooking pots over charcoal braziers, or shaping chapaties between their hands, the flat cakes of unleavened bread that with rice were their staple diet. Among them was Durga, warming goat's milk for her baby's corn mash. He crawled around beside her, his fat brown face wreathed in smiles.

Andhra touched his dark curls, asked his mother to pass on the message to Cook, and turned away. The scene could not have been more commonplace or peaceful, yet the remains of the bonfire, still visible, added an outré touch.

"Don't forget to listen for the signal and pack a few necessities," the Major reminded her as he left the bungalow for his long day's duty, after a hasty meal. "I'll be back before dark, without fail."

After their brief morning duties, chief of which was to give Cook his orders for meals, along with some rupees, so that he could go off to the market for supplies, the girls decided to do that all-important packing right away. And concluding that it was better not to let the servants know what they were up to, they picked out two boxes from the spare room and carried them to their bedroom themselves.

"Now what are the most vital things?" Jenny murmured.

"Nightgowns, underwear, toilet things, and a spare gown," Andhra decided, "and of course towels."

They packed the larger one with all they could cram in, then tied it with strong cord. Afterward they rifled the Major's chest of drawers for necessities, stuffing them into the small container. When this, too, was tied up, they both breathed a sigh of relief.

"Now if we're besieged in the fort for any length of time, we shan't have the discomfort of soiled clothes with nothing to change into," Andhra said.

Jenny nodded, adding, "I don't suppose you'll agree, but, personally, I wish we were all in the fort now. All the army families together with husbands and fathers. It would save a lot of anxiety, especially for mothers with young children."

Andhra shook her head. "We can't wish for that, Jenny. It would mean the worst had happened and our own Chandipur troops had mutinied. If that *does* occur, we'll have only the white soldiers in the fort to rely on, and they're greatly outnumbered. All we can hope is that by some miracle the ghastly tide passes us by."

"You are right, of course, but the watching and waiting is quite dreadful. I feel I shall crack soon under the strain," Jenny sighed.

"Cheer up. Maybe Mark Copeland will ride over today. I'm sure he's growing as fond of you as you are of him."

Jenny blushed, and after lunch sat hopefully on the veranda, but no one came riding in at the gate. The compound was quite deserted, the servants having skimped their work and disappeared, probably to the bazaar for news.

She grew despondent as the hours slipped by.

"I hope all's well at the railhead," she murmured anxiously.

And at the palace, Andhra reflected, fingering her amulet. Jenny was growing up at last, but still not mature enough to experience the heights and depths that shattered her own emotions at the mere thought of Prince Ranjana, she surmised, which was just as well at this trying time.

The Major arrived at last, tired and grave, though he said little. Immediately after the meal he retired for a brief rest, and the evening followed the same pattern as the previous one, he doing the bulk of the night watch.

"We can't go on like this for long," Andhra said again the following morning, seeing his weary face.

"I doubt if we'll need to," he said. "Major McQueen and I are seeing the Colonel this morning, to ask if plans can be made for outlying families to sleep at the fort tonight. It seems the best arrangement under the circumstances."

With this hope to sustain them, they got through the day in slightly better spirits. And one glance at their father's face when he walked in that evening confirmed that his plea had been granted.

"Yes, girls. The families living well out are to sleep in safety tonight, guarded by British soldiers," he told them. "One of the dormitories will be put at your disposal. You will only be sleeping there, of course. We'll return here for bath and breakfast."

"What a relief! We packed those necessities, by the way," Andhra said. "Two boxes of them."

"Good. You won't need those tonight, of course. Only if the worst comes. Just bring your nightwear and bedding rolls."

Dinner was a more cheerful meal than of late. With Ashoka coming in and out to serve them, any serious conversation was taboo, so they kept to trivial topics or discreet silences.

Andhra watched the Indian's face closely when her father gave the order for the carriage to be brought round at nine o'clock, as they would be sleeping away from the bungalow tonight, hoping to catch some flicker that would give a clue to his emotions, and whether he was glad or sorry at the way events were shaping up. But the coffee-colored face remained utterly impassive, giving nothing away.

It was a wrench to leave everything behind except their nightgowns, not knowing what they might find the following morning. When Jenny remarked on it, the Major shook his head.

"Homes and possessions are more replaceable than human lives, my dear. I'm taking the weapons. They may prove more useful than anything in an emergency."

With Patch frisking around them at this unusual late outing, they climbed into the waiting carriage. Nayan's face was as mask-like as Ashoka's, so nothing could be gleaned from him.

Andhra craned her neck toward the bungalow of the two old priests as they passed, wondering if they, too, were availing themselves of the fort's sanctuary. There was no glimmer of light anywhere, so perhaps they had already gone.

Then the light from the picket house showed faintly as they drew level with the path leading up to the horse compound and the native barracks. The sentry box was deserted, but at the sound of the carriage wheels, a couple of sepoys appeared. Instead of giving a respectful salute, they stood with insolent grins on their faces, and flung a jeering laugh at the retreating vehicle.

"Traitors!" Andhra muttered, while the Major's hand flicked to his sword hilt as though in anticipation.

Presently the great fort was reached. They descended at the gate, gave instructions to Nayan to be there at six the following morning, and went inside.

"This is the dormitory given over to the women and children," the girls were told when they reached the sleeping quarters of the white soldiers. "You'll find it rough and ready, with no privacy, but that's a small price to pay for peace of mind. You'll be well guarded here, and I'll be in a nearby dormitory with other officers, so you may sleep untroubled tonight."

They found themselves in an austere room with a score of charpoys ranged along each side. These were Indian wooden-frame beds with webbing, bleak enough to look at but adequate with a bedroll. Having brought their own, the girls flung them down and glanced round.

Some of the beds were already occupied by sleeping young children, their older brothers and sisters being all away at school in England, while half a dozen mothers stood in a knot discussing the turn of events in subdued tones. Among them Andhra recognized Mrs. McQueen, wife of the regimental surgeon, and went across to join her.

Though thin and frail-looking, she seemed cheerful enough

because her servants still remained loyal and her ayah had come into the fort with her and was sitting cross-legged on the floor by the children's bed.

Soon, conscious that they must be up early, the women drifted to their chosen places, opened their bedding rolls, undresssed, and lay down. Mosquito nets were an unprovided luxury here, but the dormitory was large and airy enough to be hopefully free of the pests.

Patch, whining at the door, reminded Andhra that he had not yet been let out for his brief run.

"If he isn't let out, we risk his disgracing himself before morning," Andhra said, "But I don't care to turn him loose alone in this vast unfamiliar place. He might get lost. Fortunately, I've not yet started to disrobe, so I'll go with him. I'll be back in five minutes."

All was quiet outside, with the last carriage gone. Dim shapes of sentries moved here and there, and only the moon lighted the mighty walls and soaring towers that had stood for centuries.

"Time to come inside now, miss," called a masculine voice. "We are about to lock the ladies' dormitory and post a sentry there."

The voice seemed familiar. Turning, Andhra saw that her memory had not betrayed her. It was the dashing young Captain John Ravenswood, who had danced three times with her at the ball and seemed quite taken with her.

At the same moment, he recognized her, striding forward and taking both her hands in his.

"Miss Andhra, I declare! What a pleasure that we meet again, though one could wish the circumstances were less grave. However, knowing that you are there in the dormitory will make the task of guard duty so much lighter."

"You are very gallant, Captain."

"Not at all. Just very glad to welcome such a charming young lady to the regiment. Let us hope that when this trouble blows over we shall become good friends, at the least."

"And how do you rate our chances of its blowing over without affecting Chandipur, I wonder?"

He shrugged. "One can only hope. The Colonel is convinced that it can never happen here. The officers, including your father, think differently. The situation is on a knife edge, but whatever happens, we're ready for it, having had more warning than the poor devils in Meerut."

"Yes, thank heaven." Suddenly she remembered Mark Copeland, and Jenny's interest in him.

"You don't happen to know if all is well at the new railhead, I suppose? Mr. Copeland hasn't called lately as he did earlier. He was rather expecting trouble."

"Why, no, Miss Andhra. We've been far too busy here lately to spare a thought for anyone not connected with the regiment. But I'm sure we can trust him to do the sensible thing. If his gang turns ugly he'll seek refuge with us, no doubt."

"I hope so. He seems a rough diamond but true-blue British. Between you and me, my sister Jenny seems taken with him."

He laughed. "So long as *you* remain aloof I shan't mind."

The inference was clear. Andhra suddenly realized the impropriety of this tête-à-tête, alone out here in the dark with a young officer all too aware of his own eligibility and not lacking words to take advantage of it.

"I must go in!" she said hurriedly. "I only came out to give the dog his run. Jenny will think me a long time."

She called to Patch, bid Captain Ravenswood a brief good night, and sought the safety of the dormitory.

He was quite a man, she reflected as she undressed, with his scarlet uniform and deep tan. Almost as handsome as Prince Ranjana. This last thought said it all, really. Now that she had fallen so hopelessly in love with the Prince, no man would ever quite measure up to him.

On this bittersweet thought, she drifted off to sleep, with Patch curled up contentedly by the side of her bed.

The girls were up and dressed by six the next morning, having decided to wash when they reached their own bungalow. The communal ablutions here were just too primitive for their liking.

They all, including the Major, looked better for their undisturbed rest, and were glad to find Nayan waiting outside for them as ordered.

Inevitably, their spirits were raised as they drove home, and even the sight of the unaccountably deserted picket house could not dampen them too much.

They were pleased to find the bungalow exactly as they had left it, with the house boy there to bring water and the cook preparing breakfast in the servants' quarters. After a wash and a change of clothes, they started on the chapaties and eggs with more appetite than of late, and rose from the table in quite good spirits.

Then the Major had to dash back to the fort, leaving the girls to get through the long day as best they could. How they would have welcomed a caller, but neither Mark Copeland nor either of the old priests turned in at their solitary gate and the morning dragged.

The dhal which Ashoka carried in at tiffin time was left untouched. They ate only a little papaw and drank cup after cup of refreshing Darjeeling tea with lemon.

"Now what do we do!" sighed Jenny.

It was only two o'clock. They had not yet acquired the siesta habit, and had no inclination for reading or needlework today. The atmosphere was stifling, and as yet there was no sign of the monsoon.

They drifted out to the veranda, with its covered roof, and stared out at the parched compound, quivering in the burning haze.

A song might have raised their flagging spirits. They often sang together in happier times, but just now songs did not come easily.

Whistling was another matter. Andhra had always possessed the ability to whistle like a boy. She fell back on her old accomplishment now, filling the veranda with the rallying strains of "The British Grenadiers," and tapping her foot to the rhythm.

Instead of giving her usual disapproving glance, Jenny now smiled in sympathy. Thus encouraged, her sister broke into the lilting swing of a polka, clapping her hands in addition.

Patch, delighted at this show of high spirits after so much gloom, thumped his tail in approval, and then began to leap about the veranda, egging her on. Jenny, not to be left out, joined in, first with a lively hum, and then by clasping Andhra's waist and hand and capering along the confined space in a ludicrous version of dancing the polka.

The exertion could not last in this atmosphere. Soon, breathless and spent, they collapsed in giggles into the cane chairs, perspiration soaking them.

"Begone, dull care!" gasped Andhra, "but thank heavens no one saw us or we'd have been certified for sure!"

And then the heavy silence, broken only by their labored breathing, was shattered by a thundering boom that rent the air and reverberated in the misty hills beyond.

White-faced, they froze, listening. Listening like the hunted deer, waiting for the tiger's roar that would tell him the stalker was close behind.

It came before the impact of the first had quite died away, a second boom sounding even more like a death knell than the first to their straining ears.

For a moment, shock held them paralyzed, unable to move or speak as the dreadful truth burned itself into their brains. Then Andhra, with a convulsive movement, sprang to her feet.

"The signal!" she croaked, in a voice that sounded far away. "The summons to the fort."

Jenny still crouched, deathly pale, in her chair, seeming incapable either of taking in the full impact of the cannon's message or of moving a muscle. Clearly Andhra must take the initiative and rouse her to the need for quick action and cool heads if disaster were to be averted.

Clutching her sister's hands, she yanked her forcibly to her feet.

"Dear heaven, Jenny, pull yourself together! If you swoon on me we'll neither of us have a chance. Remember Father's instructions. If the cannon summoned, we were to order the carriage and drive immediately to the fort."

Still dazed, with eyes dilated, Jenny clung to her sister in a stifling embrace. Only a second shock could startle her out of this numbing hysteria.

Andhra wrenched herself free and administered it in the form of a sharp slap on her sister's pale cheek.

"Don't you realize," she ground out between clenched teeth, "that the worst has happened! The signal tells us that our own sepoys have joined the rebels. The mutiny has reached Chandipur! We must run, run, run for our lives!"

CHAPTER 6

"There's not a moment to be lost!" Andhra urged, actually shaking her sister in her desperation to impress upon her the urgency. "Go and collect the two guns and ammunition while I rush round to the servants' quarters to order the carriage."

"Oh, I daren't be left on my own," Jenny croaked through pale lips, "or touch the guns while I feel so shaky. They'd be sure to go off."

Andhra had to steel herself not to lose her temper. To do so at such a moment would be fatal.

"I can't stop to argue," she ground out. "We've got to get away!"

Turning, she tore out into the blinding heat of the compound, regardless of her unprotected head. Patch dashed after her, while Jenny, like a scared little rabbit, brought up the rear.

The gate of the servants' compound was shut. Andhra burst it open and called loudly, "Nayan, you are wanted immediately."

There was no answer. The entire compound and the huddle of shabby huts were strangely silent. Surely there was *someone* around. The whole place could not be deserted in the afternoon heat. Perhaps they were indulging in a siesta.

"Nayan, come here at once," she bawled at the top of her lungs, and then, as there was still no sign of him, she called loudly for Ashoka and the other boys.

Utter silence followed. Jenny reached her sister's side and stood wide-eyed with fright, while Patch, sensing that something was terribly wrong, crouched whimpering beside them.

Andhra, with an exclamation of anger, rushed toward the

huts and beat on the door of that occupied by Nayan and his family.

"Come out, for the love of heaven!" she yelled. "We need the carriage."

The door was wrenched open to disclose the cringing form of Durga, who seemed too frightened to speak.

"Where is Nayan?" Andhra snapped. "He must have heard the gun signal. It means the mutiny has broken out in Chandipur, and we must flee to the fort for our lives."

Durga beat her hands together in a frenzy of terror.

"Oh, missy, Nayan gone to bazaar. All the men go to bazaar, and the women also, I think. I stay behind with my sleeping baba."

Never had Andhra felt such angry frustration.

"Cowards! So they desert us in our hour of need, knowing we have little power left. Is there no one at all to hitch up the horse and drive us to the fort?"

Wringing her hands again, Durga passed rapidly along the row of doors, knocking and calling. There was no answer.

"Wretches!" Andhra ground out, almost beside herself with anxiety. "We must do the best we can ourselves, though we've had no experience of stable work."

"Missy," the Indian woman exclaimed, "I sometimes help Nayan. I know how to fasten horse in carriage. But Durga cannot leave baba to drive you to fort."

"Then I shall have to manage that part alone," Andhra said impatiently. "Quick, Durga! There's not a moment to lose. Our lives may depend on speed."

The baby was now heard crying from the hut. For once Durga ignored him and ran with Andhra to the stables.

With Jenny's help, they dragged the carriage from its shed, led out the horse, and backed him between the shafts. Andhra held his head and spoke soothingly to him while Durga fixed harness and straps, with Jenny's willing but inefficient help.

"What about the boxes of clothes!" the latter exclaimed when the task was finished.

"And the guns!" added Andhra. "They're even more vital."

"Missy go and get them," Durga urged. "I stay with horse. If I leave him, maybe he bolt. He nervous."

"Bless you, Durga! You're worth all the rest put together." Andhra cast her a grateful glance, then sped back to the bungalow. Jenny and Patch at her heels.

"I doubt if we can carry them out to the carriage," Jenny panted as they reached their target. "The big one will be too heavy."

"Good heavens, yes!" Andhra stared in dismay at the neatly corded box. When packing it, she had evisaged obedient servants to answer calls as usual and bear it out for them. Now the wretches flouted tradition and did as they pleased, leaving them to cope alone.

They tugged at the box between them. It seemed as heavy as lead.

"We'll never get them both, plus the guns, round to the servants' quarters," Andhra said with sinking heart.

"Then we must leave them. Bring the guns and come," her sister urged. "We're wasting too much time."

"But after all that careful packing! Think of the days, weeks maybe we could be incarcerated in the fort!" Desperately Andhra racked her brains for some solution.

"Quick!" she exclaimed at last. "Help me untie the cords. We'll take fewer things."

They tore and hacked at the cords with embroidery scissors, brusing their hands and breaking their nails, then flung open the lids of the boxes. Without pausing a second, Andhra snatched out an armful of whatever came first to hand and flung them onto her bed, while Jenny did the same with the smaller box holding the Major's things.

"That's about as much as we can manage between us," Andhra declared when a sizable mound had accumulated. "Now you catch hold of the two bottom corners of the counterpane, Jenny, while I take the top two. That way we can lug it outside between us."

They crammed on their hats and seized the precious guns, then dragged the bundle outside, thankful that the bungalow meant they were already on the ground floor. They could never have heaved it downstairs.

With perspiration pouring from them, they dragged it to where Durga still stood holding the horse, in spite of the louder wails of her baby from inside her hut.

"Bless you," Andhra panted, hastily tying the four corners of the counterpane together. "Now help me get it into the carriage, Jenny."

Fortunately, in this climate, the carriage was open. Together, with a mighty heave, they landed the bundle into the capacious well, both now bathed in sticky perspiration. It ran blindingly into Andhra's eyes as she carefully deposited the guns beside the bundle, and watched Jenny and Patch settle themselves on the back seat.

Now came the daunting realization that she would be forced to mount the driving seat perched up front and drive past the native picket house, at the mercy of any sepoy who happened to be about. As she recalled the jeers they had been forced to endure lately on every encounter, the prospect turned her blood cold.

There was no help for it. With a silent prayer, she swung herself up into the exposed perch and took the whip in not quite steady hands. But just as she was about to give the word of command to the horse, Durga gave a joyous shout.

"Missy, missy, here come Nayan now!"

He ran up, panting and sweat-streaked. "I was at bazaar when I hear gun," he gasped. "I run all the way back."

"Well, thank heaven for that! We've lost far too much time already."

Reprimands were useless. Andhra was too thankful to be spared the ordeal of driving, for with the horse to control, she would have been quite unable to handle a gun as well, and they would have been entirely without protection against any violence that could ensue.

Thankfully she scrambled into the seat beside Jenny, relinquishing her perch to Nayan.

"Drive as fast as you can with safety to the fort," she ordered. "We should have been off ages ago."

He flicked the whip and gave the word of command to the animal. Durga let go its head and administered a slap to its flank to goad it on.

It started off with a jerk. Andhra called her thanks and farewell to the faithful Indian woman, sadly wondering if she would ever see either her or the bungalow again. So many were being plundered and burned. So many lives barbarously cut short.

The carriage swung with a sickening jolt onto the white dusty road. Patch, sensing the panic around him, crept onto her lap, shivering violently. With unwonted impatience, Andhra thrust him toward her sister and grasped the pistol, cocking and priming it ready for action. Nothing must be allowed to impede her instant response, should it prove necessary. The lives of all three of them could depend on her cool nerve.

They soon came abreast of the priests' bungalow, scarcely visible behind the trees, and then it became clear how necessary speed and defense were. Instead of the usual serenity, the peace was shattered by excited voices and raucous shouts, while a glimpse of dark figures proved that the bungalow was already a target for the rebels.

Unless the two old men had escaped before they themselves had, they would probably be dead by now, Andhra realized with horror. Would their own bungalow be the next target?

Scarcely had they passed this hazard when another loomed up in the shape of three Indians walking toward them down the road. Were they peaceful, law-abiding citizens going about their daily business, or were they taking this opportunity to join the first rebel gang they encountered in lucrative plunder and destruction?

Andhra never found out. Nayan drove straight at them, scattering them from the horse's path to the fringes of the road, and only their angry calls followed the carriage.

"I believe we shall be lucky and make the fort unharmed," Jenny murmured unevenly.

It was too soon to be optimistic. "The most dangerous stretch is still to come," Andhra reminded her, grasping the pistol a little more tightly. "I mean the picket house, of course. We'll hope the sepoys have all deserted and gone on a looting spree, then we shan't be accosted. Drive as fast and as quietly as you can, Nayan," she murmured as the sentry box came in sight.

But at the sound of the carriage two sepoys stepped from the picket house, both of them armed. Scarcely daring to breathe, Andhra stared boldly at them, determined not to give the impression that she was afraid. Though her blood seemed turned to water and the feel of the weapon in her hand was her only comfort, she kept her eyes turned upon them with a cool, disdainful glance.

When they were nearly opposite them, one of them held up his hand and, with daring insolence, commanded them to halt.

"Take no notice, Nayan. Drive on hard," Andhra ordered through clenched teeth.

Patch, sensing the drift of things, reared up with his paws on the edge of the carriage and barked furiously at the pair, his way of trying to help them. But instead of scaring the rebels off, it only seemed to enrage them, for instantly one of the cowardly wretches leveled his musket at them and pulled the trigger.

Perhaps because they were a moving target, the bullet narrowly missed the dog, and came whistling past Andhra, so close that it actually touched the sleeve of her dress. The horror of it was almost too much for even her stout heart, but the thought that Patch had almost been slain while trying to defend them filled her with a cold rage that kept her keyed up to a semblance of calmness.

She saw the second sepoy, with a diabolical snarl, dash out onto the road and raise his gun to take aim.

He would not miss, Andhra knew with cold certainty. It was him or one of them. For this moment had her father trained her and she practiced.

Quick as a flash she leaned forward in the carriage, pointing her pistol at him, and pulled the trigger.

Afterward, the incident seemed like a bad dream. All she could recall of it was a flash, a bang, the kick of her own weapon, and the howl of pain emitted by her adversary. That, and the clatter of his musket striking the iron-hard ground, proved that her aim had found its target, but with what result, they did not pause to find out.

The acrid stench of burnt gunpowder filled all their nostrils as, startled by the noise so close behind it, the horse plunged forward and tore madly along, carrying them rapidly away from the danger spot. Only Nayan's superb driving saved the vehicle from disaster and gradually calmed and slowed down the animal.

Then Jenny was able to clutch her sister's hand in admiration. "Oh, Andy, you were wonderful! Thank heaven you are so brave! You certainly saved our lives," she said, on the verge of hysteria.

"Perhaps that is only the beginning," Andhra said somberly. "Who knows what we may be driven to if this horror goes on for any length of time?"

Her voice trailed off, her thoughts suddenly on Prince Ranjana. What was he doing at this moment? Was the palace as safe as he had hoped, or did the rebels now consider the Maharajah too much a friend and ally of the British to leave him and his palace untouched? Rich pickings were to be had in that graceful building on the hill. Would the deference of years hold them back, or would they now remember and avenge the vast difference in status? Wealth untold on the one hand, dire poverty for most of his minions.

Her anxious conjecture was broken by Jenny's hand clutching her arm. Her sister was pointing along the road, to where a solitary figure in scarlet tunic strode briskly toward them.

"Why, it's Father!" they gasped in unison. "How marvelous to see him."

Nayan, as surprised as the girls, tugged at the reins as the figure drew near and pulled up.

"Thank God you're both safe!" the Major gasped, grasping the carriage as though for support. "I've been through hell since the signal went off, imagining what might be happening to you. It seems to have taken you an age, and after all I said about speed in getting to the fort."

Their father, usually so strong and cool, looked ghastly. Perspiration streamed down his pallid face and his breath came in such gasps that Andhra feared a heart attack.

She thrust open the carriage door.

"Come, sit down quickly, Father. You look all in." Grasping his arms, she half dragged him into the vehicle, where he subsided onto the opposite seat.

"I expect you walked too fast in the heat. That and the anxiety," Jenny said, mopping his face with her handkerchief. "Poor Father, to have to go through so much worry on our account."

"What in heaven's name kept you so long, girls?" he asked when he had regained his composure. "It could have been fatal. The rebels are on the attack already. Some of them were seen coming down this very road."

"We know. We saw them at the old priests' bungalow as we drove past," Andhra said, "but truly we're not to blame for getting off late. All the servants had fled, and we had a terrible time with the horse and carriage and the boxes of clothes. I thought I'd have to drive too, but mercifully Nayan ran all the way back from the bazaar and arrived just in time to fetch us."

"It *was* a mercy, too," Jenny rushed on, "or we should have been killed at the picket house by two mutineers. Oh, Father, you should have seen Andhra! She was so brave and cool. She shot the second sepoy after the first one almost killed Patch and her. It was ghastly!"

The Major looked at his elder daughter with approbation. "Well done, my dear! Those shooting lessons paid off. You're a credit to the regiment. Thank goodness Jenny has you to take care of her."

"It was nothing. I expect the other wives are having to be even more courageous, especially those with children," she said.

Nayan now made all the speed he could, with no further incidents. How glad they were of the side track to the fort, which bypassed the town, where they would have undoubtedly run into trouble. From the huddled mass of hovels and bazaars and narrow streets behind their enclosing wall came shouts and raucous singing, and the staccato notes of gunfire. The entire town seemed to be gripped by war hysteria.

"It sounds as though the rebels are looting the shops," the Major said, "and reprehensible though that may be, it should work in our favor by drawing their attention away from outlying British bungalows and allowing our people a better chance of reaching the fort unharmed."

He was quite himself again now. Knowing that his daughters were safe and unharmed had calmed him to the cool, competent officer that he actually was.

His glance fell on the bundle at their feet, on which Patch crouched, and he smiled wryly.

"So this is all you managed to snatch after all your care in choosing the right things, is it?"

Andhra nodded, smiling in sympathy. "At least we snatched some of your clothes too, but we were too confused and rushed to see exactly what. Don't be surprised if you're landed with a dozen pairs of socks and not a shirt in sight."

"Don't worry, girls. Clothes are of no importance set against your safety. Perhaps Nayan will be able to come out to the fort tomorrow and bring some comforts to us, always supposing mutineers haven't found them first."

They were all glad to see the great walls of the fort rise up. How strong and impregnable it looked with its many towers and the massive main gates now shut and barred with white sentries posted. They were halting all carriages, and allowing British occupants only through the small side gate. The only Indians allowed to pass were ayahs attached to a memsahib with children, and a few servants with a special pass, bringing food or comforts to their white families.

The girls found themselves in a vast compound, ringed round with buildings of all shapes and sizes. Women, children, white soldiers, and minor officers were everywhere. Children wailing, dogs whining, women looking lost and grim.

Then Andhra saw a face she knew. Captain John Ravenswood, looking as debonair and unruffled as ever, gave an order for the ladies and children to follow him to the dormitory where they had previously slept.

"Hang on here a few moments, girls, while I obtain a pass for Nayan to contact us tomorrow, then I'll carry your bundle to your sleeping quarters for you," the Major said.

They sat on the bundle and waited, and by the time they finally reached the dormitory, all the beds had been commandeered, chiefly by mothers with children, and the unlucky ones sat on the floor like the ayahs.

"How crowded it is," Jenny said with dismay.

"I'm afraid so. That's because every regimental family has taken refuge here, and not just the outlying ones as before. You two were late, so no beds are left. However, tomorrow I'll try to arrange for extra charpoys to be brought in. We must squeeze them in wherever they'll go."

"Don't worry about a little thing like beds!" Andhra declared. "The great thing is that we're safely inside the fort."

"That's the spirit, Miss Andhra!" came a hearty voice, and there was Captain Ravenswood beside her, smiling down at her as though nothing were amiss and this just an everyday occurrence.

With him around, life would not be too intolerable, she felt with a slight rising of her spirits. Things could have been much worse. As she recalled the old priests' bungalow, her lips pursed. With the rebels attacking so quickly, it was unlikely that they had managed to escape in time. And even less likely that they would ever be seen again. The first victims of the mutiny on their own doorstep, it seemed.

How many more would there be before this tide of ferocity spent itself and passed on?

CHAPTER 7

"I'm glad to see you reached the fort safely, Miss Andhra," Captain Ravenswood added. "The Major was in a fine old state when you didn't turn up earlier."

"We had unexpected troubles. Are we the last, then?"

"Not quite. Mrs. McQueen and her children don't seem to be around yet, but as Major McQueen was probably at home at the time, I don't think they'll be in any difficulties."

"I hope not," Andhra said. Major McQueen, the regimental surgeon, was a popular and respected figure, according to her father.

"And Mr. Copeland. Have you seen or heard anything of him lately?" Jenny broke in. "His work gang was already causing him anxiety when we saw him last."

Captain Ravenswood shook his head. "I expect he'll turn up sooner or later, now that the mutiny has erupted here. He won't be safe out in the wilds, I fear."

Jenny clasped her hands together in an anxious gesture. Andhra felt a flood of sympathy for her and longed to ask if the palace was safe, but felt too constrained in her father's presence. Besides, it was unlikely that anyone here would know.

"Well, girls, I must leave you now and report to the Colonel," Major Hilton said. "There's a great deal of organization still to be done, meals, defense, and suchlike, so if I don't see you again tonight, sleep well. We're all together and well guarded, so I'll leave you in the capable hands of Captain Ravenswood, who has been given charge of the women and children. He'll take care of you all."

When he had gone, John Ravenswood picked up their bundle.

"How sensible of you to snatch a few comforts. A lot of them rushed here empty-handed. I'll find you a quiet corner where you can relax, and later I expect some sort of a meal will be doled out." He led the way to a corner, past family groups and ayahs sitting cross-legged, crooning to the babies in their arms.

Set down in an angle of the walls, the bundle made a clean soft seat for the girls to sink down on, but Andhra felt too restless to relax. How long would they be holed up here, she wondered, knowing little of what was going on in the outside world? If only she knew how things were at the palace.

Presently she rose, and leaving Jenny and Patch curled up on the bundle, wandered down the center of the dormitory. Being so recent an arrival in India, she knew none of the wives and children she passed, trying to settle down all on one bed to a family. She would probably come to know them all too well if the mutiny lasted any length of time, in these cramped, crowded conditions, she reflected wryly.

She reached the door just as it was pushed open to admit a bluff figure of a man carrying a flaxen-haired baby in each arm. His face was strained and weary, and behind him trailed a woman looking equally exhausted, leading a child of around four by the hand.

"Why, Dr. McQueen, how good to see you," called one of the women. "I had almost given you up. I'm afraid all the beds are taken, but conditions should improve tomorrow when they bring in more charpoys."

So this was Dr. McQueen and his family, Andhra reflected, and badly needing somewhere to put the children to rest, by the look of them. Without hesitation she offered what meager help she could.

"I'm Major Hilton's adopted daughter, Andhra," she said. "Like you, my sister and I arrived too late for a bed, but we do have a bundle filled with towels and clothes in the far corner. It's comparatively quiet, and you're welcome to put the children down for as long as you please."

"How kind of you," the doctor said with the ghost of a smile. "We in the outlying bungalows had the worst of it, I fear. I was out visiting a patient when the signal went off and, as you can imagine, went through hell trying to reach my bungalow. There I found my poor Margaret in a panic, all alone with the three children. The servants had all fled, even our ayah, whom we thought we could trust implicitly. My God, what a ghastly situation this is turning out to be."

As though her endurance had finally snapped, his poor wife burst into tears. "Who could ever have imagined they would turn on us like this?" she sobbed. "Where will it all end?"

Her tears set the child off crying too. Andhra moved hastily toward her and placed a comforting arm about her.

"You're quite exhausted, and little wonder. Do come and rest. My sister Jenny has a wonderful way with children, and presently we have been promised some refreshment."

"How understanding you are, my dear." The doctor followed her down the room to the corner, a veritable haven of peace compared to the rest of the dormitory.

"Oh, Jenny, this is Dr. and Mrs. McQueen," Andhra explained. "Like us, they had a dreadful time in reaching the fort. Even the ayah has deserted them, so we must do our best to help with the children. What a mercy we have our bundle."

"It will be a pleasure to help." With her own sweet smile that transformed her plain little face, Jenny reached up her arms for one of the babies.

Andhra wiped away the tears still rolling down the mother's cheeks, with a coaxing "Don't cry anymore now. You're among friends, and quite safe here," then thrust her gently down onto the bundle, with four-year-old Kathy on her lap.

"Now let me take the other one, Doctor. How pretty she is."

He relinquished his burden with a sigh of gratitude. "This is Milly and she's two. A contented little soul. God bless you, my dears, for your help. Now I don't feel too badly at having to leave Margaret. I'm wanted urgently in the Colonel's office to plan out our campaign for any casualties we may sustain. We must set up a hospital and organize helpers, in anticipation of casualties later on."

"You can count on me for non-skilled work, Doctor," Andhra declared as he turned away. "I took a first aid and home nursing course before coming out to the wilds of India, and nursed an aged aunt of mine, so I'm not entirely without experience."

"You're a couple of wonderful girls to have around in an emergency, I must say. Your father must be proud of you." Looking rather less harassed, he strode off to join the senior officers' conference.

Andhra squeezed in beside Jenny and Margaret McQueen. Already little Kathy had lost her bewilderment and was playing with Patch, the most long-suffering and gentle of dogs. He licked her hands in friendship as she fondled and stroked him, and presently the child had confidence enough to slip from her mother's lap and play further afield with her new playmate.

Baby Jeremy stirred and whimpered in Jenny's arms. Margaret, her composure restored, took him and strained him to her breast.

"It's well past his feed time," she said. "As he's breast-fed, he's not likely to run out of supplies, thank goodness, though lack of privacy makes it a little embarrassing. However, in a situation like this, one must shelve modesty to necessity."

"Of course," Jenny said. "In any case, this corner is not too public, and if I drape your cashmere shawl round you and the baby, you can feed him unnoticed."

Margaret smiled for the first time. "Whatever happens, I'll never forget you two girls and your bundle, my dears."

So what at first had seemed a disaster had turned out for the best, Andhra reflected, recalling their tussle with the carefully packed boxes. They would have made hard seats.

Glancing round the dormitory, she saw that all the children had already accepted the situation in the way of the very young, and were tumbling about the floor like puppies. Kathy soon joined them, leaving the others free to talk.

"Did you see anything of what was going on in the old town on your way here?" Andhra asked.

"We avoided it for our own safety," Margaret said, "but it seemed to be in a turmoil. We were forced to pass close by the palace walls, and the rebels were storming into the grounds of that, too. I was sorry to see it, because the Maharajah has always been on excellent terms with the British."

"No doubt that's why they are hounding him now," Andhra said with sinking heart, adding a silent prayer: Please, God, don't let any harm befall Prince Ranjana.

When the short dusk fell, lamps were lighted, and to the great relief of the mothers, orderlies came round with urns of tea, chapaties, and milk for the children.

"Sorry we can't do better tonight," Captain Ravenswood apologized when he glanced in, "but we should manage a cooked meal tomorrow."

Questions were hurled at him from every side by anxious mothers. Were they in danger? Was an attack on the fort likely tonight or tomorrow?

They were all answered by an expressive shrug of his magnificent shoulders and placating words to the effect that no one knew what was in the rebels' minds, so they must all wait and see while being prepared for the worst.

"He might tell me more on my own," Andhra said, springing to her feet and racing down the dormitory as he disappeared through the doorway.

She overtook him just outside.

Shrouded in the quick-falling darkness, with only a dim light here and there, the vast compound of the fort looked strange and vaguely sinister. The sentries posted around had all their attention fixed on the outer wall, so she and John Ravenswood were isolated in the gloom.

"Oh, Captain!"

He turned, saw Patch, who had scampered after her, and said. "So your pet's having his evening run again. Lucky dog!"

"Why, yes." It would never do to give the impression that she was running after *him*, yet deep down, she knew that was exactly what she was doing. Fundamentally, she longed for Prince Ranjana. This handsome officer was a substitute for her craving heart.

"I wish we knew what was happening outside, Captain Ravenswood," she rushed on.

"Just stand still a moment and listen," he said. "That will give you an idea."

Now from the far side of the towering walls floated muffled

shrieks and yells, the sharp report of a weapon, and most sinister of all, a crackling noise and, here and there on the skyline, lurid splashes of light.

"Not fire?" breathed Andhra. The calamity most dreaded in this arid, pre-monsoon period.

"Afraid so. It's coming from the outskirts of the modern quarter. There's little doubt the rebels are there in force, looting and burning the bungalows of the British."

Andhra shuddered. "Thank heavens they escaped in time."

"With one or two exceptions, Miss Andhra. The two Catholic priests have not been seen, nor Mark Copeland."

Sadness welled within her. "I wonder where the rebels will turn their attention next," she murmured.

"The fort, possibly, but we'll give them a warm reception if they come within range of our big guns. Of course, once started on the path of plunder and destruction, there'll be no force to halt them out there. It will be a case of mob rule. They may even turn on the palace. Think of the magnificent loot to be found there! And think of the decades of oppression they've suffered at the hands of their own rulers, long before the British appeared on the scene. They'll certainly have a long score to settle with the Maharajah, a loyal and open friend of the British."

At this Andhra's fears returned. The palace had no impregnable walls, no cannon, no trained British soldiers to guard it like the fort. Only a mass of menials who might easily, in fear of their lives, join the rebels and betray their trust. Indeed, according to Margaret, the palace was already in danger.

Even in the dim light, he saw her concern.

"Come, Miss Andhra. Regrettable though it would be, it does not really concern us at the moment. We have enough troubles of our own, in all conscience, although no doubt your Indian blood makes you more in sympathy with the rulers of the palace."

"But with no armed guard, they could all be slaughtered in their beds!" she protested, recalling with irony the Prince's earlier offer of sanctuary for herself and Jenny. At the time, the thought of treachery among the palace servants could not have crossed his mind. Now, by John Ravenswood's reckoning, and what Margaret had heard, it was all too possible.

He was regarding her with wry curiosity.

"Such vehemence suggests only one thing, and come to think of it, you *did* partner Prince Ranjana at dinner, and later disappear with him. I know because I wanted you to watch the fireworks with me. Can it be that you've lost your heart to him, Miss Andhra? If so, it would be understandable, but not very sensible."

"Why?" She was too vexed for subtlety or evasion.

"Surely that's obvious. He will marry some high-caste Indian maiden of his parents' choosing and live in splendor for the rest of his days. Like the lilies of the field, he will neither toil nor spin, nor ever give a damn for the unfortunate underdogs in their wretched hovels outside his palace gates."

"You are quite wrong, Captain. Although he is merely the younger son, without the authority of his elder brother, he is fully conscious of the wide gulf between rich and poor, and means to do something about it as soon as he can. We discussed it over dinner, on that very evening the mutiny erupted in Meerut. He was on the point of leaving for England to further his education then, but now, of course, that will have been shelved until this ghastly outbreak blows over."

John Ravenswood smiled wryly. "And who knows what changes it may leave when it does blow over, Miss Andhra? I doubt if anything will ever be the same again. We shall all have to adapt to new conditions. Fortunately you are young enough and sensible enough to do so. Treat the Prince Ranjana episode as the girlish dream it was, and forget it. With your irresistible charm, there'll be lots of men willing to help in that direction, not least of them myself. I was drawn to you from the first moment your father presented you at the ball, my dear. Your Indian coloring only adds to your fascination. There, I've said it. Tell me you are not vexed with me, pray."

His frankness took all the wind from her sails. All she could do was stare up into his undeniably handsome face in confusion.

Seizing his moment, he bent and kissed her lightly on the curvaceous lips beneath her elegant little nose.

"That is merely a first installment," he murmured laughingly, "and now I think you should go inside before tongues start wagging. Besides, the tea urns will be emptied before you've had a share. Good night and sleep well, and if you dream at all, dream of me, my dear Miss Andhra."

Before she could regain her breath or remonstrate, he took her arm, led her to the dormitory door, and thrust her inside, closing and locking it behind her. She was left speechless with mixed feelings.

The three McQueen children were all asleep when she reached the far corner, curled up like puppies on the bundle.

"What a time you've been," Jenny said. "I suppose you were waiting for Patch. I collected a cup of tea and a chapati for you when they came round. Sit down and have them before the tea is undrinkable."

Mrs. McQueen glanced inquiringly at her.

"How are things outside, my dear? Did you learn anything?"

More than she had expected, Andhra reflected. John Ravenswood's boldness had taken her breath away, yet she was not nearly as displeased as propriety warranted. In the absence of the moon, the stars were some compensation, so to speak.

Aloud she said, "Pretty daunting outside the fort, by the sound of things. The rebels are running riot, and setting fire to the British bungalows, by the glow in the sky. There'll be some sad sights when we're eventually able to leave the fort. Some of them will have no homes to go to."

"How awful! Now I'm glad mine is well away from town. Yours too. They may be overlooked."

Wishful thinking, Andhra reflected, recalling the scene at the priests' bungalow, but somehow it no longer mattered very much. Her mind, as she ate her frugal meal, was on the palace, so much nearer the reach of the mob, and one man inside it. For however sensible John Ravenswood's advice, Prince Ranjana could never be wholly erased from her mind. Even if the mutiny shattered her world and his, and they were destined never to meet again, he would always remain in her heart.

In the crowded, darkened room, when later she lay uncomfortably on the floor with only her head on the bundle, she fingered the golden amulet resting warmly between her breasts, and tried to pretend that it was his hand caressing her.

CHAPTER 8

Sheer exhaustion brought sleep at last, but it was fitful and light. Andhra stirred frequently, stiff and aching in all her limbs, owing to the unaccustomed unyielding floor. She sensed that Jenny and Margaret were as restless as she, with only the three children blissfully unconscious on the soft bundle.

It was sheer hell trying to sleep in one's clothes, even without restricting stays, which she had discarded since arrival in India, she reflected. And quite ironical, considering that night clothes must surely be among the things in the bundle, snatched so desperately yesterday. But since she and Jenny were among the few who had brought anything with them, and they seemed to be in too crowded and hazardous a situation for anyone to undress, they had retired in their day clothes like the others.

"Dear heaven, I feel as stale as last night's party remains!" Margaret said, sitting up with a yawn. "I wonder where we can get a wash of sorts. Fortunately I stuffed nappies and toilet things for the baby into my large knitting reticule and slung it over my arm before leaving the bungalow. I was too terrified to think of anything else."

While she busied herself with feeding and changing the baby, Jenny and Andhra tidied the two little girls, combing their flaxen hair and freshening their hands and faces with a sponge moistened with toilet water. They did the same for themselves, and though still frowsty beneath their clothes, were at least able to face the world.

It was then that Andhra, glancing toward the door, saw Major Hilton peering in and beckoning to her. Thankfully she and Jenny hastened toward him.

In the morning light, he looked bleary-eyed and weary.

Evidently the weight of responsibility on the shoulders of the senior officers had been too great to allow of much rest. But he mustered a smile as he pointed to Nayan, standing waiting in the compound alongside a handful of other faithful servants who had obtained passes the previous evening.

"Treasure trove, girls," Major Hilton said. "Nayan has thoughtfully brought along a few cooking utensils to help you out. Since, with our vastly enlarged population in the fort, we're going to be short of most things, they'll be a godsend when you start doing your own cooking, as I'm afraid all the ladies must, quite soon."

Tied in a cloth bundle were a kettle, a frying pan, a teapot, some cups and plates. Andhra smilingly thanked the Indian servant. It was characteristic of him, she reflected, to think of cooking pots before anything else, since so many lower-caste natives possessed nothing beyond a few utensils, and prized them accordingly.

"Cooking our own food sounds fun," she said, "that is, if we have any food to cook."

"Basic supplies will be doled out presently," her father said, "along with chapaties that are being baked in the mess kitchen. Thank God we had the foresight to store up as much food as we could when we realized what probably lay ahead."

Nayan now stepped forward to ask if there was anything else they needed bringing, explaining that it was better he should leave the fort now, while all was quiet in the town.

The riotous noise outside had indeed ceased, she realized when she paused to listen. Sated by loot and pillage, the rebels were evidently taking some rest. Nayan was quite right. It was better for him not to be seen by them leaving the fort, openly allying himself with the British, or it might provoke an attack on him.

"Yes, lots of things," she told him, "if you can get them here unharmed. A small hip bath, a pail, and two boxes half packed with clothes in the bedroom. And if you can buy any clothes for small children, Mrs. McQueen would be most grateful, I'm sure."

Diving into her pocket, Andhra brought out her purse and thrust some rupees into Nayan's hand.

He departed, promising to do his best, but uncertain when he would again reach the fort. He would have to take care and watch for an opportunity.

"Now I guess the first necessity is food," the Major said. "You must all be ready for breakfast."

"A cup of tea right now would be heaven," Andhra sighed.

The Major pointed to a covered well in the center of the compound, with a hand pump on each side to draw up the water.

"There you are then, water and a kettle. I'm sure it's not beyond your ingenuity to build a fireplace with some of those stones over yonder. There's no lack of fuel."

Her glance following his pointing finger, she saw with satisfaction a pile of stones left over from some building project and, quite near it, an open shed stacked with charcoal and wood.

"Take care where you build it," he warned. "Jenny, come with me and I'll give you a supply of matches and tea."

Andhra, spirits rose. Now they could be independent where drinks were concerned. Joyfully she hurried over to the stones, and one by one carried four large flat ones to an open space near the pump. Visions of picnics by the riverbank back in her English school days rose up before her as she knelt, regardless of her gown, and placed the four stones to form a well. Next she brought charcoal and thin sticks, feeling very glad that here they did not use the native fuel, which was simply dried cow dung, giving off an unpleasant smell when it burned.

She had just finished arranging her campfire when Jenny appeared with the matches and tea.

"Fill the kettle while I light up," Andhra said, able to raise a smile now.

By this time, some of the other women and children had drifted out into the compound, glad of some fresh air after the crowded room. They watched with interest as the kettle was perched on top of the glow, applauding the initiative of the two girls.

How pathetic some of them looked in their bedraggled gowns, unwashed, and with hair straggling down their backs. They had been too long in this land of cheap labor and become totally dependent on servants' ministrations for every need. Now, without their ayahs and house bearers, they were as helpless as the babes in arms among them. In contrast, Andhra and Jenny were still young and adaptable enough to fend for themselves and even find it a welcome challenge.

Soon their kettle was boiling. They brewed up and set it on the glowing charcoal again, glad to be able to help Mrs. McQueen, who had now appeared with the children.

None of her servants had turned up with any aids. "They've no doubt plundered the bungalow and fled," she said sadly, "and I did think I could rely on Ayah."

They were in the act of pouring out when orderlies appeared bearing a pile of chapaties. "Tea is being served in the dormitory, ladies," they said.

"We're independent," Jenny laughed, "but we'll be glad of some of your chapaties."

Andhra was biting into the thin crisp bread when she saw her father approaching, accompanied by Major McQueen, anxious to see how his wife and children had survived the night. Behind them strode John Ravenswood.

"Why not join our picnic," she urged, "and you too, Captain Ravenswood. There's enough tea for all."

How splendid he looked in his scarlet jacket, the morning light glinting on his bright buttons and shining boots. He evidently reciprocated the admiration, by the glance he cast upon her.

"Alas, Miss Andhra, there's nothing I would like better, but unfortunately I'm on duty, making sure you are all as comfortable and well fed as circumstances allow," he said, adding, "I can see you and your sister are not going to be a burden on us if you can help it."

His glance took in her dark hair rolled tidily into its chignon, and her unfussy muslin gown, in marked contrast to the elaborate frills and furbelows of the older women.

Andhra beamed. Approbation from such a man was stimulating, to say the least, even though they were of different race and coloring.

He passed on. The two majors accepted cups of tea, but declared themselves too busy to linger.

"Calm prevails at the moment," Major Hilton said, "but not for long, I fear. It is too much to hope that the fort will go unattacked. They'll try to wear down our resistance by every means in their power. It could be a long struggle, if help doesn't reach us, and from where could that come, with so many garrisons besieged at once and all crying out for reinforcements?"

"Well, we'll do our best not to let you down," Margaret McQueen said, "but in such cramped quarters, with insufficient beds, it is going to be a strain, I confess, especially for those with babies."

"We know that, my dear," her husband soothed, "and are doing something about it. A few small rooms are being cleared and rigged out with charpoys. They'll be allocated to mothers with babies presently. You'll certainly qualify for one."

"Splendid, but if Andhra and Jenny can go in with me, so much the better," Margaret declared. "They were so good to me yesterday evening, I don't know how I should have survived the night without them. And they are so helpful with the children too, now that I have no ayah."

"Why, that's a splendid idea," the doctor enthused, "and should be no problem. Just leave it to me."

As he and Major Hilton turned away, Jenny called in a forlorn voice to ask if anything had yet been seen of Mark Copeland.

Her father shook his head. "Nor the two priests," he admitted sadly. "I fear they have come to some harm."

It was a blow to her. Andhra tried to cheer her, without much success, and she was glad when presently a room was given to Mrs. McQueen, and they could all set about making it as habitable as possible and forget other matters.

It was furnished with four of the native charpoys, which with their bedding rolls made quite comfortable couches. Mrs.

McQueen and the baby would make do with one, Kathy and Milly with another, leaving one each for Andhra and Jenny.

In addition there was a small wooden table and a couple of chairs, with coconut matting on the floor.

With much giggling the girls dragged their bundle from the dormitory, unpacked towels, nightware, and spare clothes, and stacked them on a shelf.

"With our private bathtub, if Nayan manages to get it here, we'll do well enough," Jenny declared.

The lull outside continued all morning, welcome enough to the women and children but a source of unease to the officers, who feared the rebels were plotting their next move and would strike sooner or later. When Andhra demanded to know how they stood, John Ravenswood admitted that all the Indian sepoys had deserted and their only defense now was the British contingent in the fort. "Woefully inadequate against such numbers, I fear, but stouthearted, well trained, and with plenty of weapons, including the great cannon of the fort. And of course, the fort itself is a splendid bastion in which to make our stand," he ended.

Whether the sepoys feared these great guns, or were waiting to be joined by other mutineers before they made an attack, no one knew. They could only wait and work to strengthen their position.

And then, in the late afternoon, something happened that cast horror over the entire fort.

The sentries up in the watchtower reported that a group of rebels had approached the fort and stood talking among themselves about a hundred and fifty yards off. Whether they were appraising the situation or discussing tactics was uncertain, but when dear old Colonel Rawlings was informed, he jumped to entirely the wrong conclusion.

Having been in India for all his adult life, working closely with Indian troops, he loved them like children. In the past, they had fought fearlessly under his command, during the Punjab wars and in the Khyber Pass. He had always been tremendously proud of them, and refused to believe that his own regiment would basely betray him. They had merely been swayed by false counsel and a few anti-British fanatics into hotheaded action, he declared. The moments of madness past, they now realized the enormity of their conduct and were ashamed of what they had done. They wanted to tell him so and receive his forgiveness, but dared not come too close for fear of retribution.

He would go out to them, hear what they had to say, punish the ringleaders, and overlook the lapse of the rest.

The officers grouped about him in the compound were strongly against the idea.

"If you must speak to them, sir, do it from the vantage point of the lookout," Major Hilton urged.

The Colonel would have none of it. He would meet them halfway and so dispel their fears.

"I shall ride out to them as they are used to seeing me," he declared. "Have my horse saddled at once."

"Then we shall all support you by walking behind you in a body," Major Hilton insisted, his hand fingering the hilt of his sword.

"No!" thundered the Colonel. "I go alone, or at the most, take only Major McQueen with me. They have enormous trust in the doctor, the healer of wounds. The sight of him will assure them that we come in a spirit of forgiveness. If cover is needed, the lookout will supply it."

Andhra could sense how perturbed her father was, along with the other officers. They could not share the Colonel's blind trust. But neither could they disobey his command. In silence they were forced to watch while he mounted his horse, and with Dr. McQueen beside him, faced toward the gate.

The guards opened a small side gate only, closing it immediately he had passed through. Major Hilton, anxiety etched clearly on his face, dashed to a small iron lookout grill in the great gate and peered through, Andhra beside him.

What followed was like a scene from a horror play. As the silver-haired old colonel rode at a measured pace toward them, the half dozen mutineers closed ranks and faced him. Then, when he had covered more than half the ground between them, as one man they raised their muskets and fired a volley straight at the advancing figures.

A groan went up from the horrified onlookers at the fort, followed by the sharp reports of the lookout guns retaliating. Scared by this no doubt, the rebels turned and fled, leaving two still figures on the ground, and the horse writhing in death throes.

In shocked silence, Andhra fell back to where Margaret McQueen stood as though turned to stone.

"Are they hit, wounded?" she quavered. "Let me go to them, for God's sake!"

"No one else is leaving the safety of the fort except for a retrieval party," Major Hilton said flatly. "See to it, Captain Ravenswood."

The devastating truth burst upon her then. With eyes wild as a madwoman's, she opened her mouth and shriek after shriek rang through the stunned compound.

"Take her inside, Andhra," Major Hilton said through clenched teeth, "before the bodies are brought in. My God, what an ending to the day!"

He was as near to tears as she had ever seen him.

One on each side of her, Andhra and Jenny led her unresistingly to the room they had so cheerfully taken over such a short time before. She was like a sleepwalker, stunned into suspended consciousness by this sudden and terrible calamity.

The two small girls were playing happily on the floor with Patch and a ball, the baby whimpering on the bed. Andhra placed him in his mother's arms and sat down on the bed beside her, her own arm close about the pitiful figure.

"Shall I make a cup of tea?" whispered Jenny, as being the most helpful thing she could think of.

Andhra nodded, her thoughts suddenly going off at a tangent to the Colonel's wife, a frail old woman of around sixty, broken in health by years of battling against the extremes of the climate and tropical diseases. Who would break the news that she was now a widow and would never sail for England and retirement with her Henry?

Fortunately for Margaret, with the tea came the assistant

medical officer to administer a sedative, and soon she had slipped into kind oblivion, lying pale-faced on the rough bed.

Andhra and Jenny fed, undressed, and put the children to bed in a mechanical sort of way. The whole fort was stunned and silent, scarcely able to take in the fact that their colonel was dead, as well as their beloved medical officer, and that now the leadership must fall on Major Hilton's shoulders until this somber period played itself out. What would be the outcome, no one dared to conjecture.

When Margaret surfaced to a sluggish consciousness the following morning, Andhra observed her apprehensively, fearful of what her reaction might be. However, the bereaved woman showed none of the hysteria she had suffered the previous evening. Dry-eyed, and strangely apathetic, she referred neither by word or by deed to the tragedy, but set about the baby's needs as though nothing had happened. To spare her feelings, and by necessity of the hot climate, the two victims had been interred during the night in a secluded corner of the fort, to await a more fitting burial at a more appropriate time, with full military honors.

To Andhra's joy, Nayan put in an appearance early on while all was quiet outside the fort. The carriage had been stolen by looters, he said, but in a bullock cart he had brought the precious bathtub, a pail, the two boxes, and some Indian baby clothes for the McQueen children.

"What is going on outside?" she asked eagerly.

Nayan said the rebels were scattered around the town running wild and plundering where they pleased.

"What of the palace?" she urged. "Are the Maharajah and his family still unmolested?"

Rolling his eyes, Nayan shook his head. The Maharajah had been denounced as a traitor to his own people, his palace looted and set fire to.

"What happened to him and his family?" she demanded, white to the lips.

Nayan shrugged his shoulders expressively.

"Who can say, missy? It is rumored that they were helped to escape by loyal servants when the situation turned threatening, but who is knowing the truth? All is disorder in the town."

Desolation filled her. It had been a comforting daydream to think of him there, a splendid figure in a splendid environment. Now the dream was shattered and she did not know whether he was dead or alive. Perhaps would never know.

Nayan carried the things he had brought to the room allocated to Margaret and the girls, then went off in something of a hurry, on the plea that he must get clear of the fort before he was seen aiding the Britons.

There was another reason to hasten his departure, they discovered when they opened the two boxes, for, to their fury, they found them absolutely empty.

"The sly wretch!" Jenny exclaimed. "He must have known by their lightness that they were empty. Do you suppose he ransacked them himself or one of the other servants?"

"What does it matter now?" Andhra sighed. "We're not likely to see him again. As things are, I suppose we can count ourselves lucky that he did as much as he has done for us. We can now have a bath and wash the children properly, and fortunately we brought quite a lot of useful things in our bundle. Think of Margaret and others whose servants deserted them at the first hint of trouble."

Margaret was holding up the little Indian garments one by one, smiling at the thought of seeing her children in them. For the moment, she seemed to have entirely obliterated the tragedy from her mind, and reverted to a childish acceptance of things that was vaguely disturbing. It suggested that the shock had clouded her reason, and that she would never be quite the same again.

CHAPTER 9

The following day dragged by and still the expected attack from the rebel sepoys outside did not come. Major Hilton, now in charge, did everything he could to prepare for it. The white soldiers in the fort, around one hundred and twenty men residing in the barrack block, were set to reinforce any doubtful spots round the walls with sandbags and other such essential measures. The assistant medical officer, Captain Rainham, had the isolation ward crammed with charpoys to form a casualty ward when the inevitable attack came, and called for volunteer nurses to man it. Andhra and Jenny were among the first to offer their services, and others followed suit.

"The food situation could become critical if we are holed up here for any length of time," their father confided to them during that endless day. "It will have to be rationed, I'm afraid. The threat of running short of water is even more alarming. Great care must be taken not to waste it."

Andhra sighed. Life had suddenly become dreary, menacing, and bleak, without even the consolation of her dream of Prince Ranjana, for now that he had been driven from the palace to limbo, how could she picture him, vital, virile, and deeply in love with her? He might so easily have been murdered by a rebel sword.

There were other problems. Lady Rawlings had been so shattered by the slaughter of her husband, the Colonel, that she had entirely lost her reason and slipped into a fantasy world. She wandered around the compound searching for her dear Henry, inquiring of all and sundry if they had seen him.

Margaret McQueen was little better. From a childlike acceptance of fate, she had now developed a loathing of the present situation and everything that had brought it about, so deep as to amount to obsession. All she wanted was to escape from India. To return to England and her girlhood home in a Sussex rectory where she had been happy and carefree.

Even Jenny had the additional sadness of not knowing what had happened to Mark Copeland and whether he was dead or alive, since with the wires dead, they could make contact with no one.

The assistant medical officer was deeply concerned for both the bereaved wives, especially Margaret, a young mother.

"Lady Rawlings has had her life at least," he confided to Andhra, "but Mrs. McQueen is still young, with the heavy responsibility of three young children. If she can't be got away from this environment, anything might happen. She could even take her own life and that of the children, in the belief that it is their only way to escape."

"Jenny and I will do what we can for her and the children," Andhra promised, "but we, too, are very worried about her."

For Jenny, at least, a little miracle happened the following morning. She and Andhra were out in the compound, making a mush of dhal, as lentils were called, for the children's breakfast.

While stooping over the hot charcoal to stir the mixture, Andhra heard a strangled cry from her sister. She glanced sharply up, fearing some new calamity, but the sight that met her gaze was just the opposite. For there was Jenny, laughing and crying in the same breath, and clasping the hands of a man who had just entered the compound, as though she would never again let him go. A tall, broad man, dirty and unkempt, swathed in a native dhoti and tunic that had once been white, with grizzled unshaven face beneath the turban wound round his head. At first glance he was just another seedy native, but with the perception of love, Jenny had penetrated his disguise and instantly recognized him as the missing Mark Copeland.

As the truth flashed upon Andhra, she rose and hurried toward them.

"Why, Mr. Copeland, how good to see you! We've been quite anxious about you when you didn't turn up after the signal," she said. "Where have you been holed up?"

He grinned feebly. "It's rather a long story, and if you don't mind, it will keep for a few minutes. I scent tea and food, and they'll be more than welcome, I can tell you."

"Only dhal mush and chapaties, I'm afraid. Father has rationed us. He's afraid the supplies will run out if the siege continues."

"Very wise. They sound like a feast to me."

He washed hands and face at the pump, then joined the two girls, Margaret, and the children in their frugal meal. They had scarcely finished when Major Hilton and Captain Ravenswood strode up.

"I've just been given the report by the sentries on your escape and arrival here," the Major said, shaking his hand warmly. "We all feared you had perished in the uprising. Now you must tell us all about it, and anything you can about what is happening outside. We don't know a thing beyond the local outbreak, with communications all severed."

The two new arrivals squatted down beside him. Mark Copeland drained his cup and began his story of escape.

When the signal gun had been fired from the fort, announcing the mutiny of the Chandipur sepoys, the news had spread like wildfire to the railhead, in the mysterious way of the East. The Indian track layers, already dissatisfied with the low pay and poor conditions imposed by the East India Company, were in the right mood for any spark to inflame them. They turned on Mark's two overseers in a body, using picks and shovels as weapons in place of the firearms they did not possess, and totally outnumbered as they were, the two loyal Indians were quickly slaughtered and their guns confiscated by the rebels.

"But how did *you* manage to escape?" Jenny asked breathlessly. "I should have thought you would have been their first target."

"No doubt I should have been," he explained, "but fortunately I was out of reach at the time, a few miles further off, on the last stretch where the branch line was to run to the river. I was surveying the scene for an advance camp, with a couple of working elephants and their mahouts to uproot trees."

"What a stroke of luck," the Major said.

"Indeed. Well, knowing nothing of what had happened at the railhead, I set off to walk back along the jungle trail, leaving the elephants at work. My gun was at the ready as usual for any hostile creature that might slink from the jungle, and that without doubt helped to save my life. I'd only gone about half a mile when a couple of track layers confronted me, obviously coming to find me. As soon as I saw the guns they brandished, I realized what had happened, and that my assistants must be dead. One of the rebels fired at me, but not being a practiced shot, his bullet went wide. Realizing it was their lives or mine, I fired and killed him at close quarters, then before I could take aim at the second one, he lunged himself at me and brought me down with a blow from the butt end of the rifle that dislocated my shoulder."

Jenny clasped her hands in horror.

"I guessed my end had come," Mark went on, "and so it would have proved but for Akbar Bannerjee, our engine driver. He worked on the completed section of the railroad, hauling up supplies to the railhead for the track layers. He was utterly devoted to me ever since I'd saved his life by prompt attention when he'd been bitten by a snake."

Mark Copeland paused, then went on. "When the track layers went on the rampage and turned on the overseers, he was horrified, and even more so when two of them set off in the direction I'd gone, with the avowed intention of finishing me off too. Discreetly he shadowed them, and when they confronted me, was close enough to deal my assailant a deathblow when I was at his mercy on the ground."

"Fate was on your side," Andhra said, feeling the amulet hard against her breast, and wishing that Prince Ranjana still carried it with him, now that he was in grave danger himself.

Or was he already dead?

Thrusting away the unbearable thought, she forced herself to listen as Mark continued. "With my gun shoulder useless and a mutinous gang in charge at the railhead, it would have been fatal to return there. It seemed equally risky to make for the fort until I could find out how things were in the town. My best course was to lie low for a while, but where? Then Akbar recalled the bales of straw he had recently hauled up to the railhead for the elephants. The beasts had transported and stacked them well beyond the camp on this jungle trail, ready for the advance camp. They would make an ideal shelter for me to lie up in, he decided.

"We walked back together to where they lay, feeling safe now that the light was fading. Akbar built them into a capital refuge, manipulated my shoulder, and made a sling out of his turban. I felt fairly safe there, even though we could hear the voices of the rebel gang in the distance. It was close enough to the railhead for Akbar to sneak out to me with food and water under cover of darkness.

"'The gang will not stay long, now that they are murderers,' he said. 'They will be off to the town before they can be caught and punished, then you can go in safety, sahib.'"

"Brave man," Jenny said with shining eyes.

Mark nodded. "He kept me going for the next day or two, until the gang finished the liquor and decided to get well away from the scene of their crime. They'd have killed him as a traitor had they found out. I'm truly grateful to him."

"How is your shoulder now?" Major Hilton asked.

"Painful and stiff, but it will improve with time, no doubt."

"How did you manage to reach the fort safely with the town swarming with rebel sepoys?" Andhra asked.

"Well, Miss Andhra, I waited until dusk before setting off along the railroad. I walked all night, and met no one, but knew that it would be much more risky in daylight, so when dawn came, I hid in the undergrowth until it was again safe to venture out. Then I made my way toward the town."

"It must have been hazardous once you reached Chandipur, even in darkness."

"Yes, even though Akbar had given me these Indian clothes as a disguise. There were plenty of rebel sepoys about. I had to slink along in the shadows and take a roundabout route to the fort. I had fears of finding it surrounded, and not being able to get in, but surprisingly I found few natives in the vicinity."

"They backed off in fright after killing the Colonel and Major McQueen," Major Hilton said bitterly, "but they'll be back, without any doubt."

"You still haven't told us how you stormed the fort," Jenny pointed out.

Mark grinned. "I slunk around until I found a section of the walls that was quite deserted. It was just under a lookout post. I managed to attract the attention of the sentries without making any noise. They almost shot me at first in these clothes, thinking I was up to no good, until I convinced them that I was as British as they were. Then they let down a rope ladder and hauled me up. I made my report to the officer on duty, had a brief rest, then came out in search of breakfast."

"All too brief," Major Hilton said, glancing at his haggard, unkempt face. "It's bath and bed and a visit from the M.O. for you, my lad. You can come in with Captain Ravenswood and me. We'll fix you up with clean clothes, and you'll make a welcome addition to our fighting ranks, once the balloon goes up here. But first give us some idea of what the rebels have done to the town."

Mark shook his head ruefully. "From what I could gather, there's been some burning and wrecking. No doubt daylight would reveal a pretty lurid picture. They've even turned on the palace. The sky was lit up with flames from it on the hilltop."

"We know," Andhra said in a strangled voice. "Pray heaven the Maharajah and his family got safely away before they began pillaging it."

Captain Ravenswood cast a shrewd glance her way. Was he glad that the way now seemed clear for him? Jenny wondered. With her own newfound joy, she hoped passionately that her sister would speedily forget her ill-fated prince and find some consolation with this handsome officer.

"I wonder if Delhi is safe. Have you heard anything?" Major Hilton asked, rising.

"Yes, just before the railroad communications were cut, and it's quite appalling," Mark said, hauling himself wearily to his feet. "After that bloody Sunday of May 10 in Meerut, when the three Indian regiments mutinied and murdered all the British men, women, and children on their way to church, the sepoys, athirst for more carnage, marched and rode all night toward Delhi. As you know, Delhi had no British troops stationed there. Only a few East India Company officers and civilians and three regiments of Indian infantry. In theory, the old Mogul emperor, Bahadur Shah, ruled the city from his rambling palace, but the Company had virtually filched all his power, a fact which rankled with him and his sons."

Major Hilton nodded.

"Well, when the first rebels from Meerut appeared and forced the Rajghat Gate into the city, old Bahadur Shah capitulated and joined them, leaving them free to use their knives and swords on any British they could find, as well as the few Indian Christians. The last report I had from the Company clerk was that Bahadur Shah had been proclaimed sole ruler of Delhi by the rebels, with a salute of twenty-one salvos from the Red Fort."

A groan went up from the listeners. Things were even worse than they had feared.

"So now, cut off by lack of communications, we're quite in the dark regarding how far the trouble has spread," Major Hilton said.

"Quite, but I'm afraid they would not stop at Delhi. Oudh Province has been in a state of unrest for some years. It's inevitable that it, too, will now be rebellious, which means the entire country between here and Calcutta could be hostile. Under those conditions, the Company resources will be entirely inadequate. They can't send reinforcements everywhere at once. Some of us must try and hold out until help can reach us from the south. As far away as Madras and Ceylon even."

"A hell of a prospect, if you'll pardon the expression, ladies," Captain Ravenswood broke in. "It's going to be hard on the families." His glance was on Andhra, as though he would protect her with his life from anything and everything.

Especially poor Margaret, Andhra thought sorrowfully. Her one aim now was to escape from here.

The three men now went off to their quarters, to allow Mark Copeland to clean up and rest, and to discuss tactics. Hearing her father asking Mark about any concentrations of sepoys he might have noticed on his way to the fort, she guessed that he was becoming impatient of this stalemate, and thinking of sending out attacking sorties, with the purpose of putting the fear of God into the rebels, and so, perhaps, inducing them to surrender.

Later that morning, Major Hilton spoke to the entire concentration in the fort about his plans.

"We can sit here doing nothing," he said, "ever fearful of a surprise attack and our food and water giving out, or we can send out raiding parties to wipe out as many as possible of them. To let them think we are afraid of them, and that they now have the whip hand, is in my view a dangerous thing."

All the officers and men agreed with him that his plan offered the best hope of deliverance, and that the first sortie should be made that night. All were eager to take part and have a go.

The ladies had a definite part to play, he told them. They must forget their former roles as memsahibs with servants, who never lifted a finger to help themselves, and back up their menfolk for their very lives.

Andhra was given a bale of thin canvas, from which small bags must be cut and stitched to hold powder and shot for the guns. She set to work enthusiastically as chief cutter, and before long found her thumb and forefinger chafed and sore with the unaccustomed pressure. The others fared little better. As they had no thimbles and were quite unused to such coarse materials, their fingers were pricked and their patience exhausted. Only the knowledge of their desperate plight kept them going through the long, humid afternoon. For now black clouds had rolled up, and a violent thunderstorm heralded the monsoon, which, while it would alleviate the water shortage, would make other difficulties.

When a stack of these small bags was completed, John

Ravenswood came out to collect them to be filled with powder or shot, for loading the big guns in the bastions when needed. He lingered longer than necessary beside Andhra, contriving to touch her hand and caressing her so boldly with his eyes that she felt quite embarrassed. Yet he looked so dashingly handsome in his scarlet tunic that, in spite of herself, she felt her heart fluttering in response, and was infinitely glad of his presence.

Being an officer, he managed to evade the coarse work of stitching sandbags, on which many of the men were engaged. She could not imagine him ever soiling his hands with anything. Such a lordly figure was born to command others, though whether he would emerge unscathed from their present plight was problematical. She found herself fervently hoping that he would.

He looked highly elated when he came round to the large dormitory where the ladies were working for the second time to gather the small pouches.

"Action at ten o'clock," he said with a grin that showed a flash of white teeth, "and I confess I'm not sorry. This waiting to be attacked like a sitting duck has no appeal at all for me."

"But won't it be dangerous?" Andhra said quickly. "The sepoys are so numerous."

He laughed. "My dear Andhra, danger is a part of every soldier's life. We expect it when we sign on, and would find life tame without it. Pray don't distress yourself. I've faced equal odds on the North-West Frontier and come through unscathed. I wanted to lead the sortie myself, but your father insists on going out in charge. Mark Copeland has given us an idea of where we'll find a bunch of rebels, although he thinks they are widely scattered. That's all to our advantage, of course. We're not likely to be overwhelmed by numbers."

At one time, Andhra reflected wryly, she would have heartily wished she were a man, so that she could accompany them. Not anymore. The warm, languorous surges of emotion that thoughts of Prince Ranjana could evoke, the thrilling hero worship that John Ravenswood's bold glances had brought to life, made her doubly glad of her sex.

"But if you like to be as gracious as the medieval ladies, I'll gladly carry your favor to bring me luck," he said, smiling down on her.

She grimaced. "In our present plight, we've neither ribbons nor flowers to toss at the feet of heroes."

"No? Then I'll settle for something that neither war nor poverty can take away from you. Something I'd like even better."

He bent lower, his lips close to hers, his eyes challenging.

"Not here, John!" His name slipped out in the stress of the moment. "Mrs. Carruthers is glaring at us from across the room, clearly outraged at what she considers a flirtation. Do behave yourself."

"So, but at last we are on given-name terms, my dear Andhra."

"Yes, and in place of a favor, you are herewith invited to dinner this evening along with Father and Mark Copeland. Pray don't expect a feast. It's merely one scrawny fowl I managed to cajole this morning, but I have it simmering outside in a big pan with rice and whatever else I could fling in. I guess it will help out the chapaties."

"It sounds marvelous by present standards. Invitation accepted." With a final soulful glance, he passed on.

Dinner later was a curiously convivial meal. With three extra men, the girls' room was packed. They sat on the beds wolfing down chicken broth and rice, fortifying themselves for the coming fray, as Major Hilton put it. Mark's injured shoulder ruled him out, to Jenny's clear satisfaction.

How empty the room seemed when they had gone, cheerful and confident, in spite of the fact that they would soon be in contact with armed rebels, and that some of the men who set out might never return and others return wounded.

Andhra found sleep difficult. She was equally concerned for both her father and John. The latter was storming his way past all her defenses, she realized dispassionately, perhaps because subconsciously she feared she might never see Prince Ranjana again. One corner of her heart would always belong to him, but a warm, pulsating woman, once quickened to a passionate awakening, could not live forever on a memory.

She seemed to have only just drifted off to sleep when, in the early hours of the following morning, the sounds of the returning soldiers roused her. Hastily she drew on her dressing gown and slippers and went out into the moonlit compound, almost afraid to draw breath until she had found out who had safely returned.

Several of the men were wounded, one of them being carried by two of his comrades. Anxiously she glanced about for her father and John until she saw them bringing up the rear. The Major seemed unscathed, but the way the younger man leaned on him brought a cry of dismay from her.

"You are hurt?" She hurried toward him and then saw the blood trickling down his face in the most lurid manner.

"What happened? Can I help?" she gasped.

"We ambushed a rebel encampment," her father explained. "We put up a good show, and those we didn't kill were put to flight. Inevitably we had a few casualties in the shape of wounds, though none killed, I'm glad to say. Fortunately we have the casualty ward ready. The M.O. will need some nursing help. Better get dressed quickly and see what you can do. Providentially you don't swoon at the sight of blood as some girls do."

Andhra rushed back to her room and flung on her few clothes, adding a white pinafore. When Jenny stirred and asked what was happening, she was told to go back to sleep. Time enough to involve her when casualties became heavy.

John Ravenswood was sitting on a bed looking rather dazed when she entered the casualty ward. He smiled wanly at her with an encouraging "With you to nurse me, I'm in clover. Truly I'll live to fight another day."

The M.O., assisted by a male nursing orderly, was attending to the lacerated leg of the soldier carried in. He glanced up briefly now.

"Welcome, Miss Andhra. It would help if you'd bathe off the blood with warm water and antiseptic so that I can see the extent of Captain Ravenswood's wound and decide on treatment," he said.

Having made herself familiar with the whereabouts of everything for just such a crisis, she soon had the necessities to hand, then steeled herself not to flinch when she took up the piece of gauze to swab away the congealed gore.

"You look as though you've been through a prizefight," she said as lightly as she could. "Luckily it's I and not Jenny playing ministering angel. She'd swoon at the sight. What caused it?"

"A glancing blow from a saber. Had I caught the full force I'd have been done for. As it is, the rebel just missed my eye. One of our contingent gave him tit for tat, however. He's one less to trouble us."

She cleared the clots but fresh blood still flowed.

"It needs stitching," the M.O. said, taking a quick look. "It's quite a gash, and so near the eye that the lid is caught. A narrow escape from blindness or worse. You were lucky, Captain."

"Even without my lady's favor," John murmured as the M.O. returned to finish his first case, calling, "Keep a swab pressed to the gash. I'll be through this one in a jiffy, then I'll start on you."

She had to stand very close to carry out the doctor's orders. Too close for composure. In spite of his wound, the sheer masculinity of him seemed to reach out and envelop her, mocking her reserve and claiming her for his own.

"Now if we were alone," he murmured with an impish grin.

"Just keep your mind strictly practical, Captain Ravenswood," she said with assumed primness, "and think of my reputation."

She was almost glad when the doctor strode over and began work. After a local anesthetic, he carefully stitched the gash, taking great pains with the eyelid.

Then under his direction she bandaged the wound. The doctor finally added a pad of gauze to the eye and completed it by clamping on an eye patch.

Andhra burst out laughing as the doctor turned away to inspect other casualties.

"Now you resemble nothing so much as a swashbuckling pirate!" she gasped. "Quite terrifying!"

"So long as I don't terrify you," he countered.

"Bed yourself down," called the doctor. "You're on the sick list for the time being."

"I'll help you off with your tunic," she murmured.

"Quite unnecessary, my dear Andhra. My arms are as capable as ever, as they were itching to demonstrate when you stood so close to me."

"Then I'll see if I can be of use elsewhere."

But the male orderly was equal to these first few casualties. Later, the situation could become more hectic.

Major Hilton then entered to see how matters stood with the wounded. After reassurance from the doctor he turned to his daughter.

"You look quite exhausted, Father," she said with concern. "When are you going to get some sleep?"

"Immediately, my dear, now that everything is under control. I've just been locking away some loot we confiscated from the rebel stronghold. Gold and silver filigree work and Indian jewelry that they've stolen from somewhere. If the owners can't be traced when all this is over, the proceeds will be divided among us all."

When *would* it be over, she wondered somberly, and how many more of them would be wounded or killed before that happy day dawned?

CHAPTER 10

A second sortie was planned for the following evening.

"Action is our only hope to break this deadlock, until we can be relieved," Major Hilton decided. "If we can inflict sufficient casualties and show them we are not afraid, they may decide to surrender."

Pray heaven that would be soon, Andhra reflected, noting with concern the despairing eyes of poor Margaret and the apathy of the three children. They had eaten practically nothing all day. Conditions were telling more on this family than on the others, for in addition to the low standard of food and the cramped conditions, they desperately missed their father. Even the baby sensed the hopelessness of his mother and cried feebly whenever he was not asleep. Andhra was increasingly worried about them all.

She and Jenny were busy over their brass cooking pots in the late afternoon, trying to make a satisfying meal out of the restricted rations they had been given. Rice simmered in one cauldron, while the other contained what they hoped would be a palatable curry.

"Father should be along anytime now," Jenny said. "I hope he managed to sleep in this heat."

It was quite overpowering. Andhra flinched away from the glare of the charcoal as she dished up the food into two large cans, perspiration streaming into her eyes and blinding her. It must be a hundred and twenty degrees out here.

They carried one each to their room.

Without punkah wallahs or fans, it was unbearably close inside. Margaret lay on her bed taking no notice of anything, the baby beside her, while the two little girls played listlessly with Patch.

"You all need food," Andhra said. "Come, Margaret dear, the men will soon be here for their meal. Sponge your face and the children's and you'll feel a little better."

Like an automaton, the widow wandered out to the pump, followed by the children. When she presently came back, she was joined by Major Hilton, John Ravenswood, and Mark Copeland. The latter was pretending to be a tiger and chasing Milly and Kathy. It was good to see them laughing like normal children.

They were halfway through the meal when excited shouting from outside shattered the evening calm. Setting down their plates, they rushed outside in a body.

The shouting came from the guards on the eastern bastion, and Andhra clearly heard the word "attack." So it had come at last. In the falling dusk, the rebels had crept up for a show of strength, no doubt in retaliation for the raid of last night, and they were about to undergo their first onslaught.

Even as they watched in the first shock of surprise, there came the staccato notes of rifle fire from beyond the walls, and one of the guards fell from his vantage point.

"Get inside, girls!" Major Hilton commanded. "It looks like being a hectic night."

"I can help with the reloading, if nothing more, with this shoulder," Mark said, dashing after him as he made off.

"I feel a useless clot, skulking behind, but I'd be more of a liability than an asset with only one eye," John Ravenswood grumbled.

"Tough luck. You can stay here and give us moral support."

Andhra took his arm to draw him back to their room, when a dreadful thing happened. Along with the soldiers who came pouring out into the compound from their barracks came the tragic figure of the Colonel's widow. Wild-eyed and wholly out of her senses, she dashed across the compound toward the enclosing wall, gray locks hanging about her face.

When the turbaned head of a daring sepoy appeared above the barred gates, she apparently remembered her recent loss, and that it was these rebels who had deprived her of her dear

Henry, for with a shriek of rage she began to shake her fist and hurl abuse at the sepoy.

As Andhra stood in frozen horror, John uttered a startled oath. "God, she's lost all sense of danger!"

Breaking away, he raced toward the stark figure but was just too late. A well-aimed shot from the sepoy caught her fair and square, felling her as she stood.

John bent to lift her. A second bullet whined toward him, plowing through his fair hair and slicing some of the skin from his scalp.

Then the British soldiers rushed across and surrounded him, and sent a hail of bullets at the sepoy, who fell with a groan from his perch.

Two of them lifted the crumpled figure and bore it to the buildings, while John, dazed by this fresh wound, staggered back to Andhra.

Behind her stood Margaret McQueen, convulsed by shudders. "Dead," she muttered. "Another one gone. Why couldn't it have been me, for what use am I without a husband?"

"Hush, my dear. You have the children to think of, you know." Andhra led her inside, followed by Jenny and John.

His fair hair was now stained with fresh blood. Jenny turned pale at the sight.

"Take care of Margaret and stay inside," Andhra ordered, "and you come with me, John. The M.O. had better take a look at your head."

The latter looked grim, having just confirmed that the Colonel's widow was beyond aid.

"Strange, how the most irreplaceable seem to go first," he sighed.

Fortunately, John's fresh wound was not severe. Some of the hair had to be cut away before treatment could be given, then, with a crisscross of plaster on the crown of his head, he was ordered to bed, "before your entire head comes a cropper," as the M.O put it.

"Better stand by for casualties," he told Andhra. "You're the most levelheaded of all the ladies. Bless your enduring Asian blood."

She could not bear to wait idly in the casualty ward, but kept taking brief excursions out into the compound to see how things were going.

Outside, it was all noise and bustle. The great gun, the eighteen-pounder, had been wheeled out to the most vulnerable spot near the gate. A pile of cannonballs stood in readiness, along with kegs of gunpowder. Its crew of four was busy and alert, waiting to spring into action at the first sign of a concerted attack from without. Sentries, guns at the ready, occupied every vantage point, while soldiers with rifles and swords kept guard all around the walls.

The first concentrated attack from the rebels came while she stood outside. With a sudden spurt, they stormed the walls at several points at once, wherever they seemed lower or weaker, swarming up and letting fly with their rifles.

John, ignoring the M.O., rushed out to help, calling to Andhra to take cover. As the big cannon opened fire on those above the gate, and others added their staccato voices from various points, Andhra retreated inside for safety, waiting anxiously for the first casualties to be brought in.

They came soon enough. Half a dozen with gunshot wounds ranging from a leg that merely needed cleaning and bandaging to a young lieutenant who had caught a blast fair and square in the chest. His condition was obviously serious. The M.O. shook his head and handed him over to a couple of medical orderlies with the advice to make him as comfortable as possible. Nothing else could be done for him in these makeshift conditions.

Soon after, he lapsed into delirium and his wild mutterings tore at Andhra's emotions as she helped to tend the less serious casualties. It was sad to think of his young life ended so prematurely.

The night, punctuated by sudden bursts of firing from both sides of the enclosing wall, seemed never-ending. Several more of the wives and daughters without children to care for drifted into the casualty ward to help in any way they could, even if only by brewing up quantities of hot tea and handing it round to sustain the wounded and those who cared for them, as well as the fighting men whenever a lull permitted them to relax for a brief spell.

But at last the misty dawn took over, the rebels retired to tend to their wounded, bury their dead, and plan their forthcoming strategy, and the besieged company in the fort were able to relax and breathe more easily.

The casualty ward serious cases had now grown to eleven, all treated as well as they could be in the prevailing conditions. The M.O., weary-eyed and exhausted, dismissed Andhra and the others who had toiled through the night to get what rest they could, while others took over.

Since neither her father nor Mark Copeland had appeared as casualties, she presumed they had come through this fray unscathed. She was relieved to find this was so when she crossed the compound on the way to her room and encountered the weary figure of the Major, looking begrimed and grim. A heavy responsibility had fallen on his shoulders with the assassination of the Colonel, and it could only grow more demanding until such time as relieving forces reached them from outside, she realized with a sigh.

They each went their way to find, hopefully, a few hours' rest.

Reaching her room, Andhra entered quietly so as not to awaken the children if they should be asleep. To her satisfaction, she found not only them but Jenny and Margaret also lying with closed eyes, having at last drifted off into unconsciousness after the cessation of gunfire.

Surprisingly, Captain Ravenswood rose from the chair in which he was sitting, his finger to his lips.

"Why, John," she whispered. "How good of you to look in on them when you might have been comfortably in your bed before now."

"They were all nervous," he murmured. "Margaret especially seemed to want me to stay. Now I'm glad I did."

"It's been a hectic night," she conceded, her eyes closing for a moment in sheer weariness.

"My poor Andhra. I wish I could do more to help you."

Eyes still closed, she felt his arms enfold her and draw her close. The hard masculinity of his body was unutterably satisfying, seeming to pass on his strength as she leaned weakly upon him, too tired to demur. What utter bliss to have a man to depend on in the terrifying world in which she now found herself.

A lover too. The kiss he pressed upon her unresisting lips was as hot and ardent as the torrid Indian sun that would presently rise to add to their troubles.

A moment's delight, then prudence took over.

"You must go, John, before you start the gossips tattling," she whispered, pushing at him with her hands.

"First say you love me and that one day you'll be mine," he urged.

Once, only a short time ago, that would have been impossible. A bronzed, ascetic face with velvet brown eyes topped by blue-black hair eclipsed all other men. He was the moon and stars in her heaven. A veritable god. Now the god had been routed by the sleeping tiger that had roared into terrifying activity. Vanished from her life, forever perhaps. How could a craving heart be nourished on the husks of memory, when a warm, vital being walked close beside her through this ordeal of fire? How could she repulse this new love, eager to fill the aching void, for the sake of a mirage?

"I think I'm beginning to love you," she murmured, and yet the face in her mind's eye was not his. "But how could it ever lead to anything permanent," she added with a sigh, "belonging, as we do, to different races?"

A last hurried kiss, and then he went, leaving her to shed her garments and tumble exhausted into bed.

It seemed too brief a time before she was roused by the chatter of the two little girls and reluctantly rose. Jenny was eager to hear how the night had gone and if both Mark and their father had escaped injury.

"Father was tired but unhurt when I saw him briefly," Andhra explained. "Mark too, I understand, though Father mentioned that he had badly wrenched his injured shoulder as a result of his gallant efforts during the night. It was pretty hectic and bloody. We bandaged a great many wounds, though only eleven were bad enough to be detained in hospital."

It went against the grain to recall those traumatic hours of supercharged activity. Of nauseating wounds and groaning men. Of noise, confusion, and uncertainty. Never again did she want to face such a night, and yet under the circumstances it was all too probable.

The rest of the day was a dreary replica of yesterday, except that Margaret had a strange, lost look about her and acted as though she no longer cared about anything at all. The two little girls had to depend on Jenny for everything, and even the baby would have been starved of both physical and emotional nourishment had not Andhra coaxed her into taking him to her breast and feeding him.

The harassed M.O. shook his head after a brief glimpse of her, and declared he would not answer for her sanity if she could not be quickly whisked away from this environment that had become anathema to her.

Such a possibility seemed remote. Escape from the fort under cover of darkness might be engineered, but encumbered with three young children, reaching far-off Calcutta, through terrain overrun by rebels, seemed an impossibility.

Would there be another attack tonight? Jenny and Andhra wondered as they stirred the brass cauldrons containing their evening meal. The prospect was too appalling to contemplate.

Mark Copeland felt certain that they must be prepared for it when he strolled out to join them, his arm in a sling.

"Once on the offensive, they'll almost certainly keep up the pressure until we or they crack, or we are relieved," he declared. "And we can't depend on early relief, since any reinforcements that can be brought in will be sent to Delhi first. The capital must be freed at any cost."

Andhra sighed as she straightened up to wipe away the perspiration that blinded her. A monsoon deluge during the afternoon had left the atmosphere unbearably humid, while being welcome from the point of view of water supplies. Every available receptacle, from bathtubs to brass water pots, had been set out to catch the precious fluid.

As Andhra's vision cleared, her glance lighted on a British guard escorting an Indian across the compound.

"It looks as though we've caught a spy," she said, "although he's not in sepoy uniform."

The others glanced in the same direction, then Mark emitted an exclamation of surprise.

"That's no spy! It's Akbar Bannerjee, my train driver from the railhead. The one who saved my life and helped me escape. I wonder what he's doing here."

He called, and Akbar, with a joyful cry, broke away from the sentry and ran forward.

"Oh, sahib, it is glad I am to see you reached the fort in safety," he said.

"You too, Akbar. Have you come to join the fray? If so, you are welcome."

The Indian nodded. "I had to come, sahib. The gang found out I had aided your escape and would have killed me."

"Thank heaven you eluded them! Now go with the sentry and make your report to Major Hilton, then join us for the evening meal and a gossip. You can give us the latest on what's happening outside."

They all felt slightly more cheerful when presently they congregated in the room shared by the girls and Margaret. The scraggy mutton and dhal was passed round with chapaties and eaten, if not with relish, at least with gratitude that they were not yet starving. Then the M.O. glanced in on them, his face grave.

"What is it?" Major Hilton asked. "One of the casualties sinking?"

"No, sir. It's a new case just come to my notice. Little Freddy Rundle, Lieutenant Rundle's son. A sudden collapse. I've isolated him with his mother as nurse."

"Isolation? You can't mean typhoid?"

"Even worse, I fear, sir. All the symptoms point to cholera."

There was a moment's shocked silence. Cholera, with its vomiting, purging, and agonizing cramps, was feared above all tropical scourges. A healthy person could be reduced to a skeleton in little more than a day, and death often followed swiftly. An outbreak in a closed community such as the fort would be a calamity indeed.

Margaret, her eyes burning in her pale face, threw down her plate and sprang to her feet.

"The fort is cursed!" she exclaimed wildly. "We are all doomed! If not by the sword of the rebels, then by a vile scourge that is even more horrible. My poor children. Give me the means to put them out of harm's way forever, Doctor, before I take my own life, for what is there to live for now?"

Mercifully, the children were all asleep in one bed. The doctor coaxed her into taking a powerful sedative, and soon she too lay at rest.

"I'd give a lot to get her away from here," the doctor said, setting down the cup of tea Andhra had pressed upon him. "Otherwise, I can see the frightful tragedy of the entire family being wiped out. She isn't responsible for her actions and will find some way to end it for them all sooner or later, if cholera or a bullet doesn't do it first."

Major Hilton looked grim.

"The hazards here are so great now that they'd be no greater for her trying to escape, if the distance to Calcutta were less. But without transport it's hopeless. Bullock carts, elephants, or camels, that's the best we could hope for, and far too slow for such a distance. They'd be discovered by rebels and killed before they got very far, even with a bodyguard."

Akbar Bannerjee's face suddenly lit up.

"Your pardon, Major, but I am seeing a way of escape."

"Really? Go on then, man. Tell us about it."

Akbar turned to Mark Copeland.

"After the railroad gang mutinied, they wrecked most of the stock. Trucks, engines, all they could lay hands on. But one they overlooked. My light engine, Golden Star, was parked in a jungle siding some way off from their camp, with the van in which you were sleeping when on location. I am thinking they forgot it before they went off to join other rebels. I am thinking it is there still."

Mark let out an exclamation of excitement. "By heaven, it offers a glimmer of hope, I must say! At least six people could be transported at a slow pace."

The Major looked skeptical.

"My dear Mark, the railroad construction at this end is only in its infancy. Nowhere near linking up with the hundred and twenty-one miles stretch from Calcutta to the Raniganj coalfield. How could that aid fleeing escapists?"

"By providing a quick way to the river Ralpur, Major. You may not know it, but one stretch of the newly laid track runs parallel with the river. It would be easy enough to transfer from one means of transport to another."

"In a terrain now probably hostile to whites?"

"What about such subterfuges as disguises and night travel, Major? Desperate situations require desperate measures."

"You're quite right, of course. But we should have to take a vote on it. Ask for volunteers."

"Without doubt Margaret herself would clutch at any straw to escape from here with her children," the M.O. put in, "and although the risks would be considerable, I should say they'd be less than if she remained here in her state of mind, particularly now that cholera has broken out. She would need at least one practical woman with her to help with the children and give moral support." His glance was on Andhra.

Andhra clenched her hands. In the present crisis, private desires counted for nothing. She must not think of herself.

"If it offered the best hope for Margaret, I would volunteer," she said slowly, "though it would be awful leaving Jenny and Father behind in this situation."

"You would not need to leave me," Jenny declared bravely. "I'd volunteer too. The children are more used to me. I can do almost anything with them."

Major Hilton was obviously moved. "Bravely said, my dears. As a matter of fact, I'd give a lot to see you both safely out of here, in view of the horror stories of what happened to young girls when Meerut was overrun. As for me, I've had my day, and if I'm destined to fall in defense of the fort, that is an honorable end for a soldier. Now, regarding the aspect of maintaining the engine, and providing protection for the women and children, how many men would be required?"

"Two for the engine," Mark declared. "A driver and his relief, and then there is the constant boiler replenishing and the gathering of wood for fuel. Three men would be better than two."

"Would you volunteer to drive, Akbar?"

"Yes, Major. My engine is my life."

"And I, being of the railway, would volunteer as his assistant," Mark declared. "My shoulder is not so bad as to render me useless."

"That leaves a third man needed, and who better than myself?" John Ravenswood said, his glance on Andhra. "With my injuries, I'm not much use to the regiment at the moment, but I could help out an escape bid in many ways. Shoot game to keep us in food, carry water for the engine and our use, and give some protection with my rifle to the party."

The Major nodded. "And then, if you reached Calcutta, you could stress the urgency of our position to the Company and return with reinforcements. That, I fear, is our only hope, outnumbered as we are."

Joy welled up within Andhra at this unexpected turn of events. Though unsought by Jenny or herself, it looked as though both of them would have the support of the men who figured so prominently in their emotions, should this desperate escape bid come off.

"It's better that we decide here and now, while we are quiet and free from attack, then if the decision is made, present it to Margaret in a positive way when she wakes. She'll be a different woman once away from the fort, dangers notwithstanding. Preparations for flight could be made tomorrow, and escape from here made when darkness fell. Even an attack on the fort would not prevent it, since the rebels would scarcely storm every side at once. They could make off from some quiet point with impunity."

So the attempted escape was agreed on, and scarcely had they come to a firm conclusion when gunfire was heard from outside, indicating another assault.

It was another disturbed night, although the fighting was not so fierce as during the previous one. Andhra helped with the casualties to the best of her ability, then retired at dawn to get as much rest as she could in view of what lay ahead.

When she rose, washed, and dressed toward midday, it was to find a transformed Margaret, alive with feverish hope. News of the escape attempt had circulated, and all the women approved. They had all been desperately concerned about Margaret and her fatherless mites, and all were eager to do anything they could to help.

During the afternoon, two of the faithful ayahs who had remained with their families in the camp came to the girls' room and proceeded to transform Jenny and Margaret as much as possible into Indian ladies. A weak solution of henna rubbed over their faces gave their skins the required shade. Their black hair was plaited and hung down their backs in the Indian fashion, and as a final touch, three enveloping saris were produced and draped about them by the skilled hands of the ayahs. Gauzy scarves were then tied over their heads, and the ayahs clapped their hands in glee.

"Our own mothers wouldn't know us!" Jenny gasped, laughing hysterically. "We look as Indian as you, Andhra."

"What about the children?" Andhra asked, her glance on the two little girls as they watched the proceedings with lively interest. "If they so much as open their mouths while we're passing through the town, their English speech could give us away."

"They must have a sedative to put them to sleep," the ayahs explained. "Leave it to us. They can then be enveloped in muslin and carried until you reach a safer place."

Some food to start them off was a necessity. Rice, sugar, lentils, tea, beans, and maize flour were brought from the precious food store and tied in three cloth bundles, then the three waited impatiently for the short dusk.

As it fell, the three men appeared. Akbar, of course, needed no disguise, but Andhra let out a peal of laughter when she saw John and Mark. Their sunburned faces were darkened still further. Turbans swathed their heads, hiding their fair hair.

They were both enveloped in flowing white robes entirely covering their uniforms and the rifles strapped to their sides.

"It may be amusing to you, my girl, but it's damned uncomfortable to wear," John said wryly. "I'll tear it off at the first opportunity."

They were all brought curry and tea by the ayahs, and though strung up, forced themselves to eat, not knowing when their next meal would be.

"Don't forget your water bottles," Major Hilton warned. "Probably your most important lifesaver."

As dusk began to fall, the two little girls were given their sedatives, which soon took effect. The baby was already asleep, and even if he wakened later would constitute no danger, being too young to talk.

It was decided that, for the sake of looking authentic, the three women must each carry a child until they had left the town behind, while the men took the food bundles. Swathed in colored cotton, nothing was visible of the children. Clutched to the bosoms of the escapees, they should arouse no suspicion.

Lookouts were keeping a sharp watch all round the fort for any sign of a rebel attack, and for the most deserted spot from which to make the escape. A sentry now appeared to report that sepoys were massing outside the main gate but that the eastern wall seemed quite deserted outside.

"All to the good," John Ravenswood said. "We can make our break through the small door there."

Saying goodbye to their father was difficult for Jenny and Andhra. The latter was convinced that she would never see him again, but bravely blinked back her tears and picked up one of the sleeping children.

Then the little procession of three men and three women trailed after the sentry toward the eastern wall, to murmured words of encouragement from soldiers hurrying to the main gate to repel the attack.

The first volley of shots was heard from that direction as they reached the wall.

"The fracas will draw any lurking rebels and all their attention to that spot," Major Hilton said as he watched the sentry unlock the sturdy oak door set flush into the great stone wall. "You are not likely to encounter anyone out here. Godspeed and God bless you all. We'll hang on here somehow until reinforcements can be sent, but for the love of heaven, stress the urgency as soon as you reach Calcutta, John."

If we ever do reach Calcutta, Andhra reflected, then the seldom used door was pushed stiffly open, they filed through, and it was closed and relocked behind them.

Now they were well and truly in limbo. On their own in the hostile town, with only luck and their wits to get them through and into a less menacing environment.

The narrow alley in which they now stood was dark and deserted, but as they made their way out from the shadow of the great walls, lights, shouts, and the beating of drums assailed their eyes and ears, together with the more deadly sound of gunfire from the far side of the fort.

"Remember, if challenged, keep quiet and let Akbar do the talking," Mark Copeland reminded them. "He's a resourceful fellow and equal to any emergency. He'll get us through if anyone can."

The girls pulled their gauzy scarves more closely about their faces, clutched the sleeping children more firmly to their bosoms, and marched in procession after the men in the accepted fashion of Indian wives. Akbar, confident in his grubby dhoti and tunic, his bundle fair and square on his turbaned head, led the way into the most hazardous expedition any of them had ever ventured upon.

CHAPTER 11

Bleak, alien, and crowded though the fort had been, it had become a second home, Andhra realized as they left the protection of its walls and were engulfed by the sounds, sights, and smells of the now hostile town. Now they were entirely without protection except for the weapons of the men.

At last the extent of the mutiny was forced home to them. Any office, shop, or house that had any connection whatever with the British had been looted, destroyed, or burned. Fires still flared here and there, casting a lurid glow on the fanatical faces and shining weapons of sepoys bent on destruction. The acrid smell of smoke from smoldering remains drifted about them, making their eyes smart and their lungs protest.

Weighted as they were, with their own clothes concealed beneath the saris and the sleeping babes hanging heavy in their arms, the girls found the going hard. The men were just as encumbered, with weapons hidden under their flowing robes and the precious bundles of food dangling from their hands. A challenge here and now would be hazardous indeed.

And even if they managed to get clear of the town, Andhra reflected grimly, there was a long jungle safari ahead that would take them most of the night before they reached the spot where Akbar's engine was concealed.

Knowing their vulnerability, the wily Indian led them cautiously, slinking along under cover of any shadow that offered itself. It was providential for Margaret that he had remained faithful and sought refuge in the fort. Without his engine to transport them and his flair in guiding them through this now hostile territory, they could never have made the escape attempt.

So unmistakably Indian was he, striding along with his bundle on his head, that passing Indians gave them not a second glance. Even John and Mark looked authentic enough in the fitful light, Andhra noted with satisfaction, while the ayahs had done a fine transformation job on Margaret and Jenny. All should be well, so long as they were not stopped and investigated, and forced to speak in their undisguisable English voices.

It was an anxious moment when the Nagpur Gate, giving onto the old quarter and the bazaars, loomed ahead. In the narrow street they were forced to pass close by and run the gauntlet of the throng of Indians, both men and women, going in and out. For as yet it was only nine o'clock, and the population still proceeded with their business by the light of oil lamps and the accommodating moon.

Andhra breathed a sigh of relief when they had pushed their way past the jostling throng without incident and were heading for the outskirts of the town. Now the road widened considerably, into an avenue lined with the flame of the forest trees. Their bright red blooms seemed symbolic of this dreadful time, all destruction and fire for the British.

Yet even here they were not out of danger. Indeed, the hazards were greater, for in the gardens adjoining the road stood what had once been attractive bungalows, many of them belonging to East India Company servants, British businessmen, or army families. The families had fled for their lives, but like feasting vultures ravening on the kill, sepoys, rebels, and riffraff could be seen picking over what was left of the contents of these once affluent homes, before destroying them by whatever means took their fancy.

Scarcely daring to breathe, the little procession filed silently past the gardens, their hearts pounding at every raised voice, every shadow of an enemy hovering around the bungalows. Then, to their apprehension, lurid flames began to rise from a pile of broken furniture in the garden just ahead. Half a dozen rebels leaped around, reveling in the wanton destruction, yelling and jeering at the top of their voices.

How they all longed to turn and flee, but to do so or even to cross the road to the other side would attract the very attention they were so fearful of. So, their mouths dry with tension, they forced themselves to walk calmly on, heads bent and eyes averted.

The flames rose higher as they drew level, casting a heightened glow on the passersby. Something about the little file, walking so sedately past, seemed to catch the attention of the looters, for one of them dashed out to intercept it, brandishing a fearsome-looking dagger.

Andhra felt her arms going so weak that she almost dropped her unconscious burden. Now came the moment of truth. It was impossible for them to pass any close scrutiny without being detected as the hated enemy and attacked on the spot. Had the escape plan been in vain? The planning and hopes doomed to failure here at the eleventh hour? Would they all be butchered on the spot, and those back in the fort never know the exact fate of the brave little party?

The sepoy grasped Akbar by his skinny arm, evidently demanding to know their business and where they were going at this time of night.

Akbar was equal to the occasion. He had evidently previously thought out an explanation should this kind of situation arise, for he answered without a trace of hesitation or a sign of fear, in quick Hindustani which Andhra could not follow.

Then turning, Akbar made a sweeping gesture to the three women behind, each carrying her still, small burden, so closely covered that nothing was visible.

She only recognized one word of his final sentence. The word was "cholera," that dreaded disease endemic in this country. It was evidently enough to frighten away the sepoy, for immediately he turned and dashed back into the garden, gesticulating to his friends to keep away.

Scarcely daring to believe their good fortune, the six walked sedately on. Only when the bungalows petered out and there were on more rebels to be seen did Andhra dare to speak and ask what Akbar had said to them.

"I told them that we had cholera in the family and that three of the children had died of it," he said with a grin. "I said that we were on the way to make a funeral pyre by the river, and that scared them off. Cholera is one of the few things they are fearing."

Laughing at his quick wit and coolness, they all praised him. Now they could breathe freely again and begin to hope that they would reach the engine.

Now the road dwindled to a dusty track which in turn petered out into a jungle trail.

"We must be moving very quietly now," Akbar said in his singsong English, "for some of the animals may be on the prowl. They should not harm us unless we are crossing their path."

Mark Copeland realized how tired the girls must be, carrying their unaccustomed burdens, and proposed a change. The three men each took a child, while the food bundles were slung on the girls' backs, leaving their arms free.

"Now you'll manage better on the long trek ahead," he said. "We can have short rests when forced to, but must push on as quickly as possible, or we'll be in for a drenching, I fear."

The rumble of distant thunder threatened a monsoon downpour at any minute. The atmosphere was heavy and brooding, waiting for the storm, and as soon as the jungle closed about them, the close humidity was so great as to be almost unbearable.

"This is going to be a hard slog for us all, but especially for you girls," John Ravenswood said, dropping back to walk with Andhra, while Akbar still led the way and Mark fell into rear guard, ready to defend them should any danger threaten from behind."

"I'll survive," she said. "Margaret is the weakest of us."

But now that they had made the break from the hated fort, Margaret, upheld by the carrot of freedom dangling before her, seemed possessed of superhuman strength, plodding on without complaint along the rough trail.

The moon gave just sufficient light for them to dimly see their way until the storm clouds rolled up, bringing a deluge that soaked them to the skin within minutes. As it was both useless and dangerous, because of snakes, to hope for shelter among the trees, they struggled on, half blinded by rain, mechanically following the dogged Indian.

The rain presently stopped as abruptly as it had started, but by this time they were all so wet that the only benefit was that the clouds rolled away, leaving a glimmer of moonlight to show the track, so that they were not stumbling along in deep gloom.

With her cotton sari clinging damply to her body and impeding free walking, Andhra felt utterly wretched. But neither she nor the others gave vent to their feelings, for only by plodding doggedly on could they hope to reach their destination before daybreak, and set off on another lap of this strange journey that they hoped would eventually bring them to Calcutta and safety.

With the cessation of the falling rain drumming noisily on the treetops, the night sounds began again. Strange harsh calls, stirrings and murmurings, sinister rustlings and movements of unseen creatures about them. Darting fireflies swooped like will-o'-the-wisps ahead, as though to lure them on along the track, now even more difficult to negotiate with its ruts filled with water.

Once a more hair-raising sound was heard from the blackness of the jungle, too close for comfort. An explosive expression of some large creature on the hunt. Instinctively Andhra moved closer to John.

"The cough of a panther," he murmured, "but he won't molest such a party as we are unless he's desperate with hunger."

Unfortunately the same could not be said of the night insects. They swarmed around in dozens, harassing without hindrance.

At last, just as dawn was lightening the sky in the east, the jungle petered out, and there, at the end of a temporary connecting rail track, stood a small, light 2-2-2 engine with a diminutive four-wheeled covered van hitched behind it.

The brave sight brought a spontaneous cheer from them all.

"Can we actually get under cover and dry again?" Jenny gasped.

Mark nodded. "Better still. I'll soon have lashings of tea for you all. This was my living van, so is equipped with the basics unless it's been looted.

"Still locked, so all's well," he said as he tried the door, then produced a key from the pocket of his own clothes beneath the disguising robe and inserted it in the rusting keyhole.

In a moment the wooden door was pushed open and they all climbed wearily inside, almost too tired to raise their legs sufficiently to negotiate the high step.

The growing light showed an interior of no pretensions to comfort. Just rough wooden walls, with a carriage lamp swinging from the wooden roof and shelves fixed at one end. At the other was a double bunk, which brought a sigh of relief from the three women.

The children, now showing signs of awakening from their drugged sleep, were laid on one of the bunks, the bundles dumped on another, and they flexed their weary muscles.

What a sorry mess they now presented to each other, Andhra reflected, with their muddy, bedraggled robes, bleary eyes, damp hair ruffled by impeding branches past which they had stumbled in the rain, and bites and scratches disfiguring their faces. She felt about as unglamorous as a field scarecrow, and was suddenly glad that Prince Ranjana could not see her in this sorry plight.

Yet perhaps he was as bad now, driven from the palace to exile with his family. Worse still, maybe he had not survived at all.

Her reaction to this thought must have shown on her face, for John, standing close, grinned through the stubble beginning to sprout on his chin and squeezed her hand.

"Cheer up, Andhra. Nothing's so bad that it can't get worse," he murmured.

"Bless you, you're quite right. Now what can I do to help, Mark?" She pulled off the clinging sari and immediately felt a trifle better.

Mark, practical and a born leader, indicated the bundles.

"Unpack those and put the contents on the shelves, please. After we've eaten, we'll sling up one of those saris across the bunk end and give you girls some privacy while you sleep."

Akbar, as down-to-earth as his master, found some dry kindling under the van, took the blackened kettle from the shelf, and went out to start a fire in a nest of stones, evidently used before for that purpose. The two little girls, now wide awake, slid from the lower bunk and pattered after him, delighted with this sylvan setting after the stark confines of the fort.

In a short time he had a kettle full of tea and was boiling some of the eggs they had brought with them. Jenny set out chapaties and butter on a tea chest outside along with some enamel mugs, and soon they were wolfing down the strangest picnic they had ever eaten.

With sunrise it was quite warm. The earth around them steamed, yielding up the moisture with which it was laden. A couple of gaudy parakeets settled on a tree nearby, watching the proceedings with great interest, while monkeys leaped and chattered in another.

They were now so weary that they could scarcely hold up. All except the children, who, having slept all night, now wanted nothing more than to play around in this strange, enchanting place, picking the flowers magically springing up after the rain and rolling around like puppies.

"Bed now, but what on earth are we to do about the children?" Margaret said, frowning.

Akbar smiled. "The memsahib need not be worrying. I shall take care of them. I must be gathering much wood for the engine. They will be helping me until tiffin time. After that I will sleep."

Mark clapped him on the shoulder in approval. "You're the salt of the earth, Akbar. Thanks for standing by us in the face of wholesale desertions. We all need some sleep today, besides which it will be much safer to move by night. We'll have all ready to take off at dusk."

"Very good, sahib." Grinning widely at the thought of working his beloved engine again, Akbar began to clear up the remains of the breakfast.

"That only leaves the baby," Margaret said. "I can hardly expect him to sleep all morning with me, can I?"

"No problem, memsahib. See what I make for him."

He took some of the packing cases lying around that had contained stores and tools, brought out in happier times by the engine, and formed them into a sturdy little playpen. A bale of rice straw scattered on the ground made a dry carpet, and inside this Margaret placed the baby.

Since he could not yet walk, he would be safely penned here until the sun rose high enough to be a menace.

"I am keeping my eye on him," Akbar promised. "When it is getting too hot out here I bring him to you."

With some bright flowers to play with, they left the baby crowing and crawling around, and retired to their cramped quarters to rest their weary limbs and aching eyes.

As she fell asleep, two pictures floated hazily through Andhra's mind. The first was of herself at the side of Prince Ranjana, queening it in the gorgeous palace at Chandipur, overlooking the squalor of the poor. With an unerring inner conviction she knew that this was only a golden dream and would never, never come true. The second was of herself as an army wife, married to John. An officer's lady, waited on hand and foot. Attending functions and polo meetings, giving dinner parties, spending the hot season at some hill station with the other wives. This picture was equally unconvincing. One had to love a man deeply to face life as a regimental wife in India with him. Besides, she was Indian, and mixed marriages were difficult. She could not seriously contemplate such a step.

Sighing, she thrust away these disturbing visions. Their position was much too precarious yet to dream of marriage to any man.

The sounds of movement beyond the flimsy curtain roused her toward midday. The men were rising, and it was time she did likewise, if only to relieve the patient Akbar of the children.

Jenny, squeezed in the bunk beside her, still slept deeply, as did Margaret in the upper berth. Soundlessly she slid to the floor and put on the safari suit she had worn under the sari.

What she would give for a leisurely warm bath in the privacy of the bungalow back in Chandipur. But it had probably been looted and wrecked by now, she reflected as she stepped outside into the brilliant sunshine.

There was Akbar, stirring a brass cooking pot full of rice on his fire, while the two little girls played with the baby in his cute little house. They all sported makeshift turbans made from strips of muslin to protect their heads. The sight brought a quick smile from Andhra.

"I see you've taken good care of them, Akbar. Now it's your turn to relax. You must be terribly weary."

He grinned.

"Do not be worrying. After tiffin I will rest. Very good curry for tiffin. Go and wash now. Plenty water in stream after rain."

Andhra wandered in the direction to which he pointed, and just within the edge of the jungle, came upon the stream. Where smooth stones made a hollow filled with clear running water stood John, naked from the waist up, vigorously toweling himself.

"How good it looks! I'd love to sit and splash about in it, but unfortunately it's too public," she said.

"Go ahead, my dear Andhra." There was a wicked gleam in his eye. "I'll keep watch and I promise not to look."

She blushed. "You're no gentleman, John Ravenswood."

"I admit it. Gentlemen have no fun. Like this, for instance."

Before she realized his intention, he had drawn her to him and kissed her full on the lips.

The chin stubble that he had not yet shaved off was rough against her face, still sore from bites and scratches, yet so great was her longing for love that she could not summon the power to draw away. His hairy chest, cool and fresh from its immersion, was like a supporting rock, while his hands fondled her back.

"One of the others might come at any moment," she protested halfheartedly.

"Who cares! I intend to marry you one day when all this is behind us, you know, so don't pretend to be a prude, which is far from the truth. You want me as much as I want you; admit it, my sweet."

His hands, grown bolder, were fumbling at her breasts beneath their single cotton covering.

"Hullo, what have we here?" he said softly.

He was fingering the amulet, warm against her skin, that nothing would induce her to part with. With a deft movement, he whipped it out, exposing the bright gold and flashing jewels to the revealing sun.

He let out a long, low whistle.

"So you've been purloining a few trinkets too, have you? Good for you. They'll fetch a tidy sum in the right market."

"What on earth are you talking about?" She snatched the amulet away from his desecrating hands, angry because his touch had defiled it. "This was given to me by someone special, as a protection."

"Someone special, eh? I can guess who. Well, let me tell you, my dear girl, that I have half a dozen suchlike baubles, and you can take your pick."

"Half a dozen?" She stared in surprise. "I don't understand."

"Remember that night-attacking foray back at the fort, where I sustained my eye injury?"

Her glance swept upward. He had discarded the dark patch that had given him such a piratical air, but there remained a lurid scar and the eyelid was swollen and red.

She nodded. "I recall Father saying some loot had been confiscated from slain rebels, but it may be ages before you all get any benefit from that, if ever." The fort could be overrun and anything of value taken before help reached the brave defenders, she reflected sadly, wondering if she would ever see her father again.

He laughed scornfully. "Do you take me for a fool? I didn't add all I found to the common pool."

"Then you cheated on the rest! British officers are supposed to have a high sense of honor. 'One for all and all for one,'" she quoted.

"I guess I wasn't alone in that. Ideals are all very well in theory, but in practice a fellow has to look out for himself. After an uprising on this scale, I can't see the Indian Army, the East India Company, or the British Raj ever being the same again. A little nest egg will come in very nicely to set me up in a more congenial occupation and a less grueling country. You'll benefit too, my dear, as my wife."

Stated badly, it did not sound attractive. This man she had thought so wonderful had slipped in her estimation. How could love be sustained without respect and trust?

It was impossible to avoid comparisons with Prince Ranjana. He had been willing to jeopardize his life and safety by taking Jenny and herself into the palace for protection. Would John Ravenswood have done the same, in his position? It was hardly likely.

Reservations must have shown in her face, for he said brusquely, "Still hankering after the colorful prince, my dear? Forget him. You're never likely to see him again. All that despotism will be swept away on this flood tide, like the British supremacy. Even if he survives, he'll never be a little god again."

Two angry spots of color flared in her cheeks. The last statement was true enough, but from his lips, in such a gloating manner, it was hard to take.

"Will you please go now? I want to wash. Akbar has food ready and then he must be relieved of the children so that he can get some sleep," she said flatly.

"As you wish. I'll leave you the towel, for what it's worth, having none of your own." He thrust it upon her and ambled off.

The water was blessedly cool. Taking the risk of being seen, she slipped off her safari suit and plunged into it with relish, splashing it about her with the greatest enjoyment. She had just emerged and was drying herself when Jenny appeared.

"Lucky for you it wasn't Mark," Jenny said. "You're growing quite bold. I shall only dare wash hands and face."

"We'll probably come to accept starker things before we're through this expedition," Andhra declared, "and be none the worse for it. Living fundamentally strips away the conventional shams pretty quickly, doesn't it?"

It also exposed people in their true light, she reflected. How would they all emerge at the end of it? Especially John.

The whole party were up and about when she reached the clearing by the engine. Margaret looked more like her old self than she had done for some time, Andhra was glad to see. Mark's shoulder was usable again, and they all looked in better spirits after their rest.

Akbar's curry sent out appetizing smells. He had already served the two little girls, and they were tucking into their food with gusto. He was also eating his own tiffin.

"Please excuse," he said with a grin. "I eat now, then sleep in my engine cab."

"He's worth his weight in gold," Mark declared, "and I can vouch for his cooking. Help yourselves, girls. It may be the last good meal we'll have for a while."

They finished as usual with lashings of tea, then Andhra and Jenny cleared up and washed the plates, mugs, and utensils in the stream, in true Indian fashion, while Margaret fed the baby.

Then Jenny and Mark wandered off into the jungle, intent on being alone for a while. John glanced after them.

"Would you care to emulate?" he suggested.

Andhra was not in tune with him at the moment, but a desire to stretch her legs while the occasion presented itself overrode her distaste.

"We might try for some game," she suggested. "I'd love to show off my shooting."

He brought the rifles and they set off.

She was reminded vividly of those jungle forages with her father while sailing up to Chandipur. How were things going back at the fort? And how was Patch taking their sudden desertion of him? A pang went through her as she pictured him lonely and fretting.

The damp warmth of the jungle closed around them, isolating them in its green dimness. Far above them, the tree branches reached out, festooned by liana vines that linked them together. Exotic orchids hung tantalizingly here and there, and brilliant, harsh-voiced birds flashed across their path, to vanish again in the undergrowth.

Underfoot they had need to tread warily on the faint trail

made by Mark and Akbar on earlier shooting forays. The uneven ground was boggy in places, now that the monsoon had broken. Strange creatures scuttled from their path. A giant centipede with its innumerable legs, a forest lizard of bright green, and once, a wicked-looking snake.

Out of sight, monkeys chattered excitedly and birds made strange calls. Andhra was so intent on her surroundings that she missed the jungle fowl that started out of a tree fern and flew erratically ahead of them. John bagged it with his first shot and dangled it before her with a derisive grin.

"When it comes to shooting, it takes a man," he taunted. "For this, too."

Setting down his gun and the bird, he grasped her with ruthless determination and kissed her with such ardor that her first thrust away from him was transformed into clinging submission.

She needed love, heaven knew, and because the man she craved was beyond reach, she grasped at the next best like a drowning man clinging to a straw.

But when he became too bold, she broke away, because the glorified image of the man she had superimposed on him could never in her eyes be guilty of crudeness.

"There's a time and place for everything, John," she objected. "Our main concern just now is to reach Calcutta safely and book a passage to England for Margaret and the children. Jenny and I must stay with her until she sails. Your task is clear enough. A return to Chandipur as speedily as possible with any reinforcements you can induce the Company to give you."

His mouth hardened. "You're beginning to sound like your father, my dear. I don't want a commanding officer for a wife, but an adventurous little woman prepared to follow me to the ends of the earth and have fun with the proceeds of what I've hidden in my tunic pockets. South Africa, the West Indies, we can go where we please and live like lords for a time at least. That's what I mean to get out of life."

In spite of the warmth, she chilled at the prospect.

"But life isn't like that, John. Not simply idle pleasure. It's the facing of difficulties and sorrows that helps us to grow up better people, I think. One must put down roots. Having chosen the Army as a career, it's up to you to make the best you can of it, and leave the good times for when you retire."

"My dear girl, how can a broken-down, middle-aged has-been enjoy life, always supposing he survives cholera, small-pox, or an enemy bullet? I don't mean to take the risk."

Words failed her, and she was saved the necessity by the appearance of Jenny and Mark returning from their stroll, Jenny looked radiant.

"Oh, Andhra I'm so happy," she burst out. "Mark has just asked me to marry him!"

"Congratulations! How marvelous. You'll make an ideal pair, and I'm sure Father will approve when he hears of it. He thinks such a lot of Mark."

Andhra was genuinely pleased that the course of true love was running so smoothly for her little sister, even if her own path was bedeviled by fate and doubts.

They walked back together and had to run the last few yards when another tropical downpour descended on them, driving the entire party into the van.

Mark set out the brass water jars, glad that they would be filled to start out with. The engine water tank was topped up too, yet he looked preoccupied enough to prompt Andhra to ask what was on his mind.

"I'm wondering what the storms are doing to the railroad between here and the river," he confessed. "It's only a temporary job for running out men and materials at this end, and without consolidation can't withstand floods. We may get through, but it will be a close shave."

"Poor Mark. I'm so glad you have the admirable Akbar to depend on."

"Same here. When he wakes we'll get ready for going. As soon as the rain stops, you girls might go out and brew up tea. A batch of chapaties would be useful too. We could make a meal of them and goat's cheese before we start, and keep the rest for breakfast."

It was a relief to have something useful to do. When the clouds passed and the sun came out, all three women set to with dry wood, griddles and kettles, and some of the crushed maize they had brought with them. John showed them how to roast the jungle fowl he had shot, wrapped in leaves and placed on a hot stone on the fringe of the fire.

"Don't you have to pluck it first?" Jenny asked with lively curiosity.

John shook his head. "When the skin's cooked crisp, it just peels off, feathers and all, leaving the succulent flesh exposed. I hope you put some salt in the food packages."

"Of course. Rice, chapaties, and everything would be tasteless without it. We had to learn the art of survival pretty fast during our short time at the fort," Andhra declared.

"You certainly do a nice line in chapaties, my dear." He filched one from the growing pile and sank his teeth into it.

She smiled to see such a cozy, domestic side of him. So different from his earlier reckless boast. Perhaps later, when back with the regiment, his sense of honor would return, and he would surrender his loot to the common pool and settle down to be a good officer again. Perhaps he would find someone happy to settle down with him, for she could not really see herself in that role.

Toward dusk Akbar emerged, rested and smiling, from his engine cab. He ate and drank heartily as they all did, then announced he was ready to drive off.

"Plenty water, plenty wood. I go now to get up steam," he declared with a huge grin.

Andhra washed and packed their few utensils, then stepped outside to take a look at this modern wonder in working order.

"Wonder" was the only word to describe her. A trim little engine painted green and black, with two small sets of wheels and one large. On the shield above the large center pair, her name stood out proudly in letters of gold, Golden Star, and beneath it the date of her release, 1855.

Smoke belched from her tall, brass-topped chimney, polluting the sylvan air but promising power to whisk them away from danger. At the other end of the boiler was attached the cab, where Akbar, protected from the weather by a sturdy metal canopy, stood feeding wood to the boiler.

"Very good engine," he said with satisfaction. "Please to come inside and I will be showing you her controls."

She took the grimy hand he extended, put one foot on the metal step, and was hauled up.

The control panel next to the boiler was most impressive, full of levers and gadgets, all brightly polished.

"You must be quite clever to have mastered all this," she said, genuinely impressed.

"All due to Copeland sahib. He is knowing many things, and a good teacher."

"And this is where you sleep when the engine is at rest, I suppose?"

Behind them was a high bunk running the whole width of the engine cab, complete with bedding roll. Shaded by the canopy, it made an excellent bed.

"That is so, and please to look below it."

One half was a large water tank, while the other housed a fuel bunker, now stocked with the wood gathered that morning by Akbar and the children.

"How compact, and no running expenses if you can gather wood by the wayside," she enthused.

"Golden Star not fussy. She will burn coal or any fuel that comes handy." He sounded as proud as though he had designed her himself.

"When you've quite finished admiring her, I'll climb up and we'll get going," Mark now called up.

Laughing, she was helped down.

"Are you driver or fireman?" she asked as he climbed up.

"We're interchangeable. I'll let Akbar take off or he may have a fit of the sulks. Actually, I've got to keep a sharp lookout for any damage the storms may have done. It won't be easy in the darkness, but fortunately there's a moon."

Reluctantly Andhra returned to the van. It would have been terribly exciting staying up there and feeling almost part of the engine when she moved off, pulsating with life, but she must be content to peer through the window, covered with mosquito-proof wire mesh, at the front of the van. Here she and Jenny waited expectantly for the first tentative jerk.

It still took them by surprise. A great belch of smoke from the engine stack, a screeching of metal, a jolt that almost flung them to the floor, then slowly and cautiously, they pulled out from the sylvan retreat to the long ribbon of the single-line track.

They were on their way to freedom.

A great cheer broke from the little party in the van. Would they make it, or would all their efforts prove in vain?

CHAPTER 12

"Since those two appear to be self-sufficient and I'm not needed at the moment, I may as well get some rest," John said when they were chugging on their way at a cautious pace because of the unpredictable conditions. "I gather we should reach the Raniganj coalfield depot around dawn, and passing through will be tricky. We'll need all our wits about us then."

Taking off only his boots, he lay down on a rough blanket at the end of the van used by the men. Andhra, Jenny, and Margaret followed suit, tumbling into the bunks fully dressed after the two little girls were settled on a blanket below. From now on until they reached Calcutta, the going would be rough and ready, she reflected.

To make matters worse for Mark and Akbar, they were no sooner well underway than another storm hit them. The water came down in sheets, drumming on the van roof, so that none of them could sleep. Jenny lay tense and nervous, conscious of the strain on the two men in the engine cab. At any moment they could run into an impediment on the track, or even a landslide in such conditions.

Andhra squeezed her hand comfortingly. "Try not to worry. Remember how resourceful Mark is, while Akbar can outwit any monkey in cunning. They'll get us through if anyone can."

When the rain stopped, they dozed a little, to the fearsome calls of stalking animals in the jungle alongside the track. Once a mighty roar made Andhra quake. Surely a tiger, hungry and enraged.

As soon as the black outside the meshed window square became gray, Andhra rose, too tense to lie longer. She would have to wait to consult Mark about making tea, since it could not safely be done in the van on the move. Fortunately, they still had plenty of chapaties left.

The light outside strengthened. Were they nearing the coalfield depot, which could be hazardous to pass through if the rebels had taken charge? Andhra peered through the small window but all she could see was the rear of the engine.

The track just here had been laid on a high embankment, probably to keep it clear of any floodwater that might accumulate at the end of the rainy seasons. At the foot of the embankment on either side she could see the jungle pressing close, but the way ahead was entirely obscured by the engine. As she stood there, it braked suddenly to a shuddering halt, almost jerking her off her feet.

The screeching brakes and the jolting of the van roused the others, the baby making fretful protest. As soon as they were quite stationary, Andhra wrenched open the van door and climbed down to see if there was any chance of lighting a few sticks and boiling a kettle for tea.

She cautiously walked past the engine on the narrow track to find both Mark and Akbar out of the cab and standing transfixed in front of the vehicle. Silently Mark pointed ahead.

There, only yards away, the heavy rains had taken their toll of the recently constructed, unconsolidated embankment by washing a part of it completely away, leaving only the skeleton rails. They stretched for about thirty feet over a complete void.

"My God, if we'd met that in the dark and the blinding rain it would have been curtains for us all," he said grimly.

Andhra blanched. "I suppose that means we'll have to abandon Golden Star. How on earth are we to travel?"

"I'll have to think that one out. Our first problem will be to get through the coal depot, now that our hopes of making a dash through it are gone."

"Are we far off?"

"Not more than a mile or so. There seems no other way to bypass it than by taking to the jungle and keeping well hidden. We're too unusual a party to pass unchallenged in daylight."

"Then we'll first need something inside us. Is it safe to light a fire and make tea?" Ever practical, Andhra realized that one problem was enough to face at once.

"Go ahead. With the line in that state we're quite cut off. Neither man nor machine can pass until it's rebuilt."

With Jenny's help, she soon had some dry sticks alight and tea made. As they drank it and munched the chapaties, the men debated their next move.

It was decided that they must find out exactly what the situation at Raniganj was and if they could skirt it at the edge of the jungle without too much difficulty. Akbar, as the only Indian man among them, was the obvious choice for this reconnoiter, so after he had eaten he set off.

They all stood by the van watching him scramble down the embankment and squelch his way through mud and water at the base until he came to the rubble of the collapsed section. Over this he scrambled with agility, and the last they saw of him was his soaked, mud-stained dhoti flapping around his thin legs as he disappeared into the jungle.

Now began an anxious wait for them all. Mark, however, practical leader that he was, kept them too busy to speculate. As soon as Akbar returned, they must be on the move again toward their goal, so far away, and so must make what preparations they could.

So for the second time the girls fastened up small bundles of food, enclosing a change of clothes for the children and the bedraggled saris, while Mark and John cleaned and reloaded their rifles and collected what ammunition was left. The water bottles, more essential than food in this climate, were filled and placed ready to sling over their shoulders, then the two men began to pace up and down, watching for Akbar's return, rifles to hand in case of necessity.

Andhra, too restless to stay in the van, joined them as the time dragged on, fervently hoping that nothing bad had befallen the resourceful little Indian who had proved himself such a staunch ally.

Toward midday, when she was beginning to fear the worst,

Mark let out an exclamation of relief. "Here he comes, pounding down the line as though he's in trouble!" he added. "That wrecked embankment is going to prove awkward. He can't get to us except by climbing down and then up again. If he's being chased that could be fatal."

He was. On the Indian's trail, not far behind, came three men, guns at the ready.

As Andhra stared in consternation, one of them took aim and fired at the fleeing figure. He missed, and Akbar increased his speed, but what would happen when he reached the unsupported rails? she wondered, wide-eyed with fear.

"He'll never get down the embankment alive," Mark ground out. "Not with three of them hounding him. So it's either his life or theirs. Take aim, John, as soon as Akbar is out of the line of fire."

The two rifles were raised as the fugitive reached the void, but instead of scrambling down the embankment as expected, Akbar, as though he had thought out the move while running, made not the slightest hesitation. With one lithe movement, he swung himself down beneath the skeletal rails and, dangling there, began to forge slowly ahead, hand over hand.

"My God, he'll never do it!" gasped Mark. "I expect he thinks he'll be a more difficult target there than on the embankment, but the lines give too little cover. Watch your chance, John, with the pursuers."

As he spoke, Mark took aim at the leading pursuer, who fell instantly.

The second man, now very close, fired at Akbar, making his desperate way across the chasm. The bullet hit one of the steel lines and ricocheted harmlessly away. John's calculated shot brought him down immediately after.

The third man was now on the brink of the chasm. He paused to take a more careful aim at the moving target ahead of and below him. Mark, grim-faced, was just about to pull his own trigger when nature came to his aid and did the job of dispatch for him. For without warning the crumbling permanent way beneath the pursuer's feet, disturbed by the gunfire and Akbar's passage perhaps, collapsed with a loud rumbling, precipitating the assailant with it as it fell and burying him in an avalanche of stones and earth.

Although Akbar was freed from the fear of death from a bullet, his position was just as desperate, for the new collapse left the two steel rails without any support at the far end, and Akbar in imminent danger of collapsing with them.

"Cling on, Akbar! You're almost across!" Mark called hoarsely, flinging himself down on the brink, ready to help the plucky Indian up to safety as soon as he came within arm's length. John, too, dropped to the track beside him, arms extended downward.

"The fellow must have muscles of steel!" he gasped.

"Thin and wiry like many Indians," Mark agreed. "Come on, Akbar, you've made it!"

Careless of his own safety, he leaned further out to grasp one of Akbar's hands, cut and bleeding from the effort. John grasped his shoulder at the other side, and together they dragged him up through the rails to safety.

Utterly exhausted now, the Indian fell to the ground, gasping and panting, and lay there for a few moments, before Mark and John helped him to his feet and assisted him into the van.

"A strong cup of tea is what he needs now," Andhra declared, pouring one from the still-warm kettle and adding a heaped spoonful of sugar.

Akbar drank it thirstily, then his cheerful grin beamed out on them all, assuring them that he was his normal self again.

Except for his hands. Andhra poured warm water into a bowl and commanded him to wash them, then anointed the cuts with antiseptic salve and bound them with strips of rag.

"We can't have our most valuable member going sick," she declared. "Now tell us what you found out on your foray."

"The coal depot along the railway siding is taken over by rebels," he said. "We cannot pass through it with safety. The town also is risky. We must bypass both by taking to the edge of the jungle."

"Did you manage to pick up anything regarding conditions

in Calcutta?" Mark asked. "Have the sepoys mutinied there too, I wonder? If so, things are going to be difficult for Margaret getting away."

"All is well there as yet, sahib. No rebellion, East India Company safe, and ships still sailing in and out of the harbor at Howrah."

"Thank heaven for that!" Margaret exclaimed.

"But all not well in many other places," Akbar continued. "Bombay, Lucknow, Cawnpore, Agra; all having much trouble, and many British killed."

"That's certainly bad," John broke in. "With our resources and troops stretched on so many fronts, our chances of getting help to Chandipur are slim. Who could have envisaged the trouble escalating to such a pitch?"

"Who indeed?" Mark sighed. "But now to our first priority, which is to get Margaret and the children to Calcutta and shipped off home. We had better get started if there's much jungle safari. We can't risk being caught out there at nightfall."

A sling had been fashioned for the baby, who was now strapped to Mark's back, leaving his hands free for the gun. The bundles were similarly slung behind John and Akbar. The latter had his machete from the van, in case it was needed in the jungle, and John a second gun.

"By the way, what made those three Indians chase and attack you?" Mark asked as they began to climb down the embankment, Andhra and Jenny helping the two little girls. "You look inoffensive enough."

"They used to be working for you on the railroad before they rebelled. They were knowing me as soon as they saw me snooping round the coal depot and asking questions. As I had not joined them in the mutiny, they considered me a traitor worthy of death. If you had not been waiting with your gun, I should be finished now. You saved my life."

"We seem to be making a habit of saving each other," Mark said with a grin. "Now you lead off with your machete, I'll come next with my gun at the ready, then the women and children, while you act as rear guard, John."

They forged ahead at the foot of the railroad embankment, keeping just the yard or two within the jungle that was necessary for concealment from above. The two children, after so much confinement, were delighted to be on the move and trotted along, chasing gaudy butterflies that crossed their paths and laughing at the squawks of the parrots and monkeys.

It was a relief to be free of bundles and burdens, if only for a brief spell, Andhra reflected. Even without, the going was hard. Mercifully they were shaded from the glaring sun, but the soaked undergrowth literally steamed, giving the atmosphere about them a Turkish-bath consistency. Underfoot, with no trail except what Akbar hacked out for them, the ground was uneven and littered with damp, rotting branches and leaves, through which they were forced to squelch their way, keeping a sharp lookout for snakes or other obnoxious creatures.

As the lethargy of early afternoon hung over the jungle, there was fortunately little fear of encountering any big game, and they reached the coal depot soaked in perspiration but unhurt. By now the embankment had leveled off to the ground, the rails had spread to several tracks accommodating coal wagons and engines, and on either side of these stood the railway ghats with their sheds and offices, and giant bunkers piled with coal.

In spite of the rebels now being in charge, shunting and other activities were taking place. This, along with the number of individuals drifting around, made concealment still expedient, and the jungle party dared only peer through the branches.

"Fortunately the village lies on the other side of the tracks," Mark murmured, "so we need penetrate no further into the jungle. We'd better push on until we're well past them both, then decide on our next move."

"Milly tired," the child said plaintively as they began to move off again.

"Hush, darling!" Andhra whispered, terrified lest any of the idlers on the ghats should overhear and investigate. "Come, I'll carry you."

They struggled on for perhaps a further half mile, plagued

by insects that the movement of their feet disturbed, then sank down in the shade of a clump of wild banana palms, too exhausted to worry about the state of the ground.

Water bottles were passed round, and chapaties munched, then John said tersely, "What now? Do we chance walking along the track? It will be a lot easier, and we can keep our eyes open for any transport we can grab."

Mark stared at him. "Are you mad? We'd soon be spotted and captured by passing traffic. This line is still working, in spite of the mutiny."

"How the devil are we to reach Calcutta then? You're surely not envisaging us tracking well over a hundred miles through the jungle burdened with infants and women, are you?"

Andhra bit her lip, not at all relishing his tone. He sounded like a spoiled child. All his charm had vanished with the adverse conditions and the unattractive state in which it had left them all. She glanced appraisingly at him. With a distinct growth of stubble, his fair hair unkempt, his uniform stained and torn, gone was the dashing officer who had almost filled the void left by the disappearance of Prince Ranjana. True, they were all in the same deplorable condition, and now was the time when only basic sound character counted and would carry them through to the bitter end. Mark's solid integrity and unfailing leadership, and Akbar's admirable good humor and grit, transcended all the difficulties and dangers besetting them these fateful days, but the same could not be said of John. Stripped of his magnificent array and commanding position, what was left? A sorry case of self-interest and surliness.

"I'm proposing no such thing," Mark said coldly. "Have you forgotten the river? It was used for transportation long before the railway was dreamed of, and is still so used by most people. If we can reach that, we stand a far greater chance of filching a boat and getting away undetected. It can't be far off, as the railroad was built roughly parallel."

Akbar grinned widely, teeth flashing.

"River not far. Two, three miles on the other side of jungle, sahib. River very good for navigation, now rains are coming. Plenty boats sailing on it to join the Hooghly River down to

Howrah. Some boats having steam now. I am working on one before joining the railway."

"The deuce you did! Good old Akbar, you'll save us all yet!" Mark again exuded imperturbability as he added, "The jungle trek won't be easy but it's the only possibility. We must try and work out the shortest way to the river."

He glanced up. Through the broad leaves of the bananas, the sun's rays fell in dappled light and shade. He stepped out into the open, studying its position for a moment.

"Since the river is only two or three miles north, we should reach it before sundown if we plunge straight into the jungle and keep the sun on our left hand," he said. "Without a trail of any sort it won't be easy, but it's our only hope."

"If we don't encounter a wild elephant or a Bengal tiger or a lurking snake first," John said dourly.

Mark almost lost his temper then. "If you're trying to scare the girls from making the attempt, you damn well won't succeed! They've more pluck than you. The danger of walking on the open track is twice as great as chancing the jungle, so shut up and try to help."

"Mark is right," Jenny said, taking her stand by his side. "I'm sure we're all prepared to follow him under cover, knowing the frightful consequences if we're captured."

"Hear, hear!" Andhra and Margaret augmented.

"Oh, well, get going then. On your own heads be it."

Since hacking a path through virgin jungle was a major task, Akbar was allowed to carry nothing save his machete. The children were taken by Mark, John, and Andhra as they pushed squarely into the matted undergrowth.

Akbar, leading the way, certainly needed both hands and no encumbrances, for almost immediately they encountered a bamboo thicket, too big to skirt, through which a path must be hacked. Insects of every description, rudely disturbed, buzzed angrily around them, biting and stinging viciously.

It was nothing short of hell. The children began to cry, and in the humid heat they were all soon soaked in perspiration and feeling like limp rags.

They were through at last, and the going a little easier, but not for long. A great black cloud rolled up, obscuring the sun, and they braced themselves for the rain.

"Now we must rely on the compass." Mark fished the instrument from his pocket as the deluge broke, drumming and swishing on the treetops and soaking afresh their already soaked clothes.

The baby, hanging heavily in the sling on Andhra's back, protested at this treatment in the only way he knew, by howling at the top of his lungs. Thank heaven they were beyond the range of human ears, she thought, pushing her tangled black hair out of her eyes.

John, walking just behind her, closed the gap. "Now do you still think it a good idea to trek through virgin jungle in the monsoon?" he growled.

"As the lesser of two evils, yes," she said through set lips. "For heaven's sake, try to be more tolerant and fall in with what Mark considers the best course. He's had plenty of experience in hostile conditions, whereas yours has been mainly confined to well-run compounds. As the leader, he should be obeyed unquestioningly if we're ever to reach our goal."

"And if we ever do, I'll take good care never to let myself in for such situations again!"

"There are equally trying and dangerous situations in the Army, such as defending the Khyber Pass."

"There's also an institution known as buying oneself out of a commission," he said grimly. "I mean to put as much distance as possible between myself and this accursed country as soon as this mutiny is put down, unless we're all wiped out first. Thank the Lord I now have the means."

Her lips curled.

"Hiding away loot for your exclusive gain is just about on a par with your general behavior lately. Aren't you afraid I'll give you away?"

"No. You're too steeped in British traditions of honor among gentlemen. You once told me I was no gentleman, remember? It still holds."

He grasped her arm, squelching through the rotting vegetation beside her.

"But I can promise you I'm a damn sight better than most of 'em when it comes to passion. Marry me and you'll never want another man, Andhra."

Angry color flared in her cheeks. "I must have been mad to ever contemplate such a thing, or to imagine myself in love with you. Jenny, now, is in a happier position, with a man to be proud of. She'll love and respect him all her life."

He laughed derisively. "That kind of steady devotion would never satisfy you, Andhra. I know you better than you know yourself. Those burning, secret desires within you need something stronger to kindle and keep the flame burning."

He was right, darn him.

"But not you!" she said with intensity.

A vision of Prince Ranjana's golden face flashed before her, dark eyes burning with that very flame. Closing her eyes for a moment, she could feel his virile form pressed against her, his arms supporting her, his hands caressing her. His sensitive lips seemed to rove her face, seeking and finding her eager mouth, as his golden talisman lay like a warm touch between her damp breasts.

She stumbled slightly with lack of care and tiredness. Her eyes flew open to find the rain petering out but conditions underfoot even more atrocious.

He pressed the arm he still grasped. "Take care. You're worn out. We all are. When are we going to reach that damned river?"

A beetle scuttled on enormous legs across her path. It was as highly colored as a Chinese vase and quite three inches long. She shuddered, and hurried to close the gap growing between her and the rest of the party.

The sight of it, as well as the boggy ground, dispelled the desire she had to rest. She pushed on doggedly with the others, the baby growing heavier and heavier with each step.

The sun came out and the jungle steamed, but now it gleamed slantingly through the trees, low in the sky. Soon it would be gone, then darkness would fall even more swiftly than usual in the gloom of the jungle.

And with darkness, the night prowlers.

Where was the river? Had Mark miscalculated in the appalling conditions? Was his compass reliable?

They all had the same fears. They were stamped on their faces.

Then presently, when the sun had quite gone and the light in this green hell was beginning to fade, Akbar in the vanguard gave a joyous shout.

"The river, we reach it!"

The ground had begun to slope downwards, but the elephant grass was denser, nourished by the life-giving moisture of the waterway during the long droughts between monsoons. Akbar slashed away with his machete and they staggered forward to emerge, miraculously, at their goal.

The sun-baked, cracked mudflats that would have greeted them before the rains had dramatically changed into the brown mudbank of a sizable waterway, flowing lazily toward the distant Hooghly River. It would gain volume and strength each day until the season changed again, and hopefully transport them to safety.

But for the moment, there was little else to raise their spirits. No boats, no shelter, and night about to fall. Evening, when the wild creatures, both benign and hostile, came down to the water's edge to drink their fill and perhaps look for an easy kill.

What could they do now?

CHAPTER 13

Once again, the resourceful Akbar proved their salvation. He had been surveying the scene and making a brief foray to right and left along the riverbank. He returned with a grin of satisfaction, pointing to the faint track on the right worn by countless bare feet.

"Village not far off," he interpreted. "The men are coming this way to hunt and fish. If we explore, maybe we find a boat that we can borrow."

"Good observation," Mark said. "It sounds our best course. In fact, the only way possible to transport such a vulnerable party. The river is flowing well now, so navigation should not be difficult. We'll have to use stealth, though. We don't want to be captured at this stage."

"Then we'll push on now," John said. "Dusk should be an ideal time to filch a boat, while the villagers are all at home intent on their evening meal."

Andhra glanced at Jenny and Margaret. They looked as worn out as she felt. The children, too, had had enough of this damp exhausting trek and needed food and rest.

"If we push the children too far they'll probably give us away with fretful crying when we get near the village," she said with decision. "What we all need is a few hours' rest, then one of you try to find a boat at dawn, before the villagers are about."

Mark nodded. "It makes sense, if we could rig up a temporary shelter. By Jove, what about those waterproof sheets enclosing the bundles?"

Anticipating just such a rainstorm as they had passed through, Andhra had encased the bundles of food and clothing in two waterproof sheets she had found in the rail van. Now they were hastily pulled off.

"If we can fix one among those bamboos, a few feet from the ground, and use the other as a ground sheet, the children at least can lie down dry and comfortable," she said.

The light was now fading fast. Hastily Mark and Akbar set to work, the latter clearing a small space among the tall bamboos while Mark fixed up an awning on the tough, light poles.

With the second waterproof spread below and the closely growing bamboos pressing round to form a screen, they had a shelter of sorts. The children were given a drink and a chapati, then lay down without any prompting and almost immediately fell asleep.

"You three huddle round the children and get some rest," Mark said then to the girls. "I shall stay on guard beside you. We dare not light a fire, but I have good ears."

"I am taking turns with you, sahib, until I go to look for boat," Akbar said, squatting down beside Mark.

John, with a few pungent expletives, flung himself down on the cut bamboos, and quite soon his snores showed that he was asleep.

The darkness was now total, yet even in this vulnerable position, Andhra felt no fear, with Mark on watch. How different things would have been had John been their only protector, she reflected painfully. He was strictly a fair-weather man, going to pieces when things were against him. Well, better to find out now. It would underline her realization that there could never be anything serious between them.

On this final thought, she too drifted off to sleep.

She awakened as the blackness was turning to gray and the mist of dawn from the river gave the only remission from the heat of the whole day. A little stiff from the cramped, damp sleeping position, she sat up to see the stolid back of Mark, still sitting guarding them.

"Oh, Mark, you haven't been on duty all night?" she whispered in dismay, moving to his side.

"Not quite. Akbar took a turn while I slept. Now he and John have gone off to see what they can spy out."

"It's quite time he pulled his weight instead of leaving all the hard work to you and Akbar."

He glanced with comprehending expression at her closed face, then his hand clasped hers, warmly comforting.

"Poor Andhra. Your romances are not flourishing in these trying conditions, are they?"

She shook her head.

"Don't blame him too much. Few of us are heroes when it comes to the test. He'll shine again when things are back to normal and he's in his old commanding position."

"But not for me," she said decisively. Mark didn't know about the hidden loot, and John's avowal to quit the Army as soon as possible, and of course she could not sink to his level by giving him away.

"I could never take him seriously for several reasons, the chief of which is that my heart already belongs to someone else," she added. "Perhaps I never cared enough about him to overlook his faults and pretend he has qualities not really there. I'm not like Jenny, for instance. She'll follow you to the ends of the earth and stick by you through thick and thin. Fortunately, you're not the sort to test her much. I'm happy about you two at least."

"Your turn will come, never fear."

She doubted it very much. Having been given a glimpse of heaven, it was going to be difficult to find it again, now that her world had crumbled about her.

The others were now awake, and as Margaret was doling out a meager breakfast to the children, Akbar's cheerful face suddenly came into view.

"Any luck, you old son of an engine?" Mark asked.

"Plenty luck. An old steamboat is riding at river's edge about half a mile away. I am thinking she was left stranded high and dry when river shrank. Now monsoon here she is afloat again."

"Does she look river-worthy enough to get us to Howrah, would you say?"

"I am thinking so, sahib. She is not waterlogged. I am

boarding her and inspecting her engine. It looks in good order."

"What a stroke of luck for us! I wonder if we can get it going and away before someone from the village spots us. Any idea how far that is?"

Akbar shook his head. "River mist too dense to see the other bank, but I am thinking village some way off, as I am hearing no sound."

"Two more circumstances in our favor. Fate seems to be on our side at last. We'd better get going as fast as we can before the sun disperses the coverage," Mark said.

Their remaining assets were hastily bundled together and they set off up the rough riverside trail.

Presently, the small steam launch loomed up like a ghost in the mist. At first glance she was neither promising nor pretty. Just twenty-five feet of peeling paintwork, faded awning, and squat funnel. Andhra could picture it belching smoke and smuts when underway, powered by its wood-burning fire.

"No doubt its owner uses it to transport goods and passengers downriver when the water is deep enough," Mark said. "That being the case now, he'll be along anytime to get her moving. We'd better beat him to it."

"Where's John? We can't leave him behind," Andhra said.

"He is going further down river track to see if he can tell where village is," Akbar explained. "He will be back at any moment."

"He'd better make it snappy then. How about fuel, Akbar?"

"Enough wood by the engine amidships to start her. We could be stopping later to gather more, after we are getting safely past village."

"Right. Climb aboard then, everybody."

It was an unpleasant business, squelching the yard or so through mud and turbid water, the children carried shoulder high. They had just boarded, and Akbar and Mark were busy amidships with the engine, when John appeared, a couple of scrawny chickens dangling from one hand and a brass pitcher of water in the other.

"Don't ask me where they came from," he said with a grin, dumping them on the bleached boards.

"Just tell us how far away the village is," Mark chuckled. "That's all we're concerned with."

"Not more than about a mile. I vote we make our getaway before they start looking for lost property."

"That goes for this old tub too. I hope to heaven the mist holds until we get safely past. The river seems wide enough to keep us safe in midstream, but coverage would be welcome."

Akbar was working like a demon, raking over the ashes and bits of dry charcoal left in the firebox. He added a few pieces of the damper wood lying around and managed to coax it into reluctant life, while Mark checked the water level and topped it up.

Once really going, it roared away. The heat from it was considerable, promising to dry their wet clothes in no time. Smoke poured from the funnel, the boiler began to sigh and snort and leak wisps of steam.

Andhra felt like cheering, but dared not add to the necessary noise of the boat. Instead, she stood with the two little girls, watching with interest as Akbar peered at the gauges, thrust more wood into the firebox, and then motioned to Mark that he had sufficient steam to get them away.

Mark, equally familiar with the working of these small steam launches, went forward and, with a heave on the windlass, proceeded to haul in the anchor from its bed of mud, the muscles rippling on his hairy arms. It responded with a squelch and a sucking noise, and was hauled aboard.

Akbar was still hard at work. A clanking noise now made itself heard, and suddenly the vessel came wholly to life, as they felt the propeller begin to vibrate beneath their feet. Mark snatched up the long fending pole and began to thrust at the turbid water, pushing the boat, with an effort that made the sweat stand out on his bristly face, out into the main current of the river.

Once out in midstream, even without power, they would have drifted slowly down river in their desired direction. With the engine now adding its weight, they moved quite briskly.

"We could do with another willing hand," Mark said. "Who'll volunteer to take the tiller?"

"Count me out," John declared. "I'm no navigator."

Andhra's lip curled. "I'll do anything to help if you show me first."

"Good girl! Look, this is the tiller, a very important part of the mechanism." He swept the iron rod over into position. "It directs our course," he went on. "You hold it steady if you wish us to go straight on. A slight movement either way, and the boat will respond by deviating to right or left. You'll soon get the hang of it, but until you do, Akbar will guide you. Listen for his instructions. Now take hold and see what you can do."

Feeling quite keyed up, Andhra squatted on the box beside him and took the indicated rod. It felt hot to the touch, but that could have been her sweating palms.

"Move it a little in each direction and see how obedient to your command it is."

She shifted the tiller rightward and felt the boat move in response. Another slight movement and they were on course again, heading steadily down midstream.

"That's fine. Keep her dead on that course until we're well past the village, and then I'll take over. Until then I must keep watch in case of trouble."

He crouched in the bows, his gun at the ready. John took rear-guard position in the stern, while Akbar manipulated the engine. Margaret, Jenny, and the children crouched under the faded awning until the danger spot should be past.

As the power of the sun began to break through, the mist was dispersing rapidly now, rising up and drifting away like curls of smoke. Suddenly the village came in sight, a cluster of hovels stretching back from the banks of the river into a jungle clearing. Broad-leafed banana palms backed a patch of cultivated ground alongside, and a few small rowing boats clustered round a wooden landing stage thrusting out into the water.

So early in the morning they might be lucky enough to pass without being noticed, Andhra reflected, hanging tensely on to the tiller. But it was too much to expect. A couple of thin brown boys, splashing naked at the edge of the river, heard the chug-chug of the engine, stared in disbelief at the marooned steamboat, now afloat with an alien crew, and dashed off to raise the alarm.

"Full speed ahead, Akbar!" Mark roared. "Give her all she will take!"

They spurted forward as yelling Indians burst from the thatched huts to leap into the rowing boats and follow. But a warning shot over their heads from Mark brought them to a full stop, and soon the steamboat had left them behind out of sight.

"I wonder how the village came to possess such an asset as a steamboat," Andhra remarked when all danger was past. "I feel terribly mean at depriving them of it."

"Don't fret. It won't belong to any villager," Mark said. "My guess is that it's the property of some small trading company plying up and down the river. It probably went too close to the bank when the water was falling at the beginning of the dry season and became marooned. The owners will be coming to salvage her now that the rains have floated her again, but our need is greater than theirs, I think."

Another need was now making itself felt. The need of food and drink. While the amateur crew pushed on at a steady speed, Margaret and Jenny set to work on the fowl John had brought in, plucking and cleaning them and setting them to roast on a spit Akbar rigged up by his firebox. They also made chapaties from their dwindling corn flour and a great kettle of tea. No further village was sighted, so when they reached a little creek, they dropped anchor within it, to refresh themselves and replenish the engine fuel.

"We are finding plenty wood here," Akbar said, "but first we eat."

The delicious smell from the roasted birds had them all drooling. Almost burning their fingers, they tore the fowl apart, distributing them round, so that even the baby had a drumstick to gnaw on and encourage his erupting front teeth. The meat, though as tough and stringy as the average Indian chicken, was consumed to the last scrap, along with fresh chapaties and mug after mug of hot tea.

After the meal, as much wood as they could find space for was collected, the brass pitchers filled with welcome fresh water from a stream flowing into the creek, and even their precarious food supplies augmented in a most welcome way by a stem of wild bananas they found growing nearby. The two little girls considered these much more fun than tough chicken and stuffed themselves until they could eat no more.

It was now time to push on. Having inspected the below-deck conditions, and finding only a dirty hold with little light or air, stifling in the midday sun, Mark decided they would do better staying on deck. But as they were bound to encounter other boats, and more frequent villages as they progressed downstream, disguise was imperative.

The three women again donned the saris and head scarves, lugged so laboriously in the bundles through drenched jungles, while Mark and John followed suit. Faces were rubbed with the bark from some tree that Akbar pounced on with satisfaction. It gave them all a deeply sallow tinge, which, though not calculated to add to their attraction, certainly added a distinctly Asian air.

"Thank God the awning survives," Margaret said when they emerged from the tree-shaded creek into the brassy glare of the shimmering river.

"It will shade you women and children during the afternoons, and you can sleep under it at night," Mark decreed. "Settle down, all of you, for a siesta and remember to keep mum if we pass anywhere near a village or another boat. Now that we're in no immediate danger, two of us can manage the boat quite easily."

The two, of course, being Akbar and Mark. John threw himself down, pulled his turban over his face, and went off to sleep, quite content to leave the hard work to others.

The following days slipped past like a waking dream. They chugged slowly past villages sprouting between river and jungle, where dhobi wallah's beat clothes on flat stones before spreading them out to dry, and women washed their precious brass pots before filling and carrying them home, perched gracefully on their shining black heads. Once the clearing was greater, to disclose a small town clustered round a tall minaret. How they itched to go ashore and buy some of the mangoes and other colorful fruit and vegetables displayed for sale in the market. Just small mounds on the bare earth, their owners squatting behind, patiently waiting for a sale. It was considered too risky to pull in close to the bank, even for Akbar to land. The steam launch, still a rarity on this minor river, would attract too much attention. Instead the women and children crouched out of sight beneath the awning until all danger was past and the jungle pressed in on them again.

The jungle gave way to paddy fields as they neared the Hooghly, where water buffaloes pulled wooden plows through the mud, making ready the ground for the rice planting that would follow the rains. Cultivated patches of maize and other crops alternated, with women bent double in the relentless sun. Sudden drenching rainstorms, which hit them most afternoons when black clouds raced up, ceased as suddenly as they began, when out would come the sun again, along with hordes of mosquitoes and equally troublesome insects. They were all bitten unmercifully on their unshielded faces, the children especially looking as though in the throes of a severe dose of measles.

"Bad enough, but it could be much worse," Margaret summed up philosophically. "Isolated on the boat as we are, we've avoided picking up cholera or smallpox, and the fresh rainwater we catch and boil has kept dysentery and typhoid away."

"True enough," Andhra agreed. "We've even been spared the malaria we might have suffered from mosquito bites owing to Akbar's wizardry with the jungle herbs he gathers and boils for us. We have much to be thankful for."

Were the others back at the fort so lucky, she wondered, especially Father? Had the cholera that had hit the encampment just before their own departure spread as it often did, or been checked by the medical officer? It was hard to know nothing at all. But perhaps better.

Yet by the time they were nearing the place where the tributary on which they sailed would join the broader Hooghly River, they were all growing weary of confinement and inadequate food. The small stock they had brought with them had gone. They had nothing now except fish they caught from the river or what they could shoot or find on the riverbanks. While passing through cultivated regions it was impossible to land in search of food, and the situation was growing desperate. They were short of fuel for the engine too, so when a tree-shaded creek suddenly presented itself, they turned the prow of the boat into it, hoping to find both.

Here, virgin jungle greeted them again, with its harsh-voiced birds and chattering monkeys. Vegetation pressed close to the life-giving water, flaunting exotic flowers and trailing snake-like vines.

A rocky space promised a landing. They dropped anchor, and the three men and Andhra landed, John, Mark, and Andhra with guns and Akbar on the lookout for both food and fuel.

"Be taking great care, and do not be straying far from the creek," Akbar warned. "This Bengal tiger country, and wild elephants also, so go as quietly as the stalking panther and keep two together."

"I'll take care of Andhra, never you fear," John said, taking her arm and leading her off.

They could hear the calls of jungle fowl, but the trees and undergrowth were too dense to see any clearly enough to take aim. They did see wild plantains and marked them down for picking on the way back.

A colony of marching termites was carefully stepped over, then suddenly they came upon a more open space. It was not a tidy, man-made clearing, but a scene of devastation, with trees uprooted and great branches torn off those left standing.

"I've seen devastation like this before when tiger shooting," John said. "It's caused by elephants, sometimes by one rogue male, driven from the herd by fellow members. Messy, isn't it, but it will provide all the engine fuel we need without going further."

They began to collect the smaller pieces and pile them up. They soon had a sizable mound, and it was then that a loud trumpeting burst on their startled senses.

They spun round to see at the far side of the devastation a large bull elephant, looking very formidable indeed. Instinctively John raised his rifle.

"They're difficult to kill at that distance," he muttered, "but it might scare him away. They're shortsighted, and he probably hasn't seen us."

The report of the gun sounded deafeningly in Andhra's ears. Nervously she clenched her hands, waiting for the beast's reaction.

It followed immediately. The elephant, downwind, picked up the hated scent of man and, with another loud bellow, charged straight in their direction, crashing through the fallen trees and branches like a moving avalanche.

Fear petrified Andhra. To her horror, she could neither move nor cry out, could only wait dumbly for the great, trampling hooves, the mighty, goring tusks.

John, more used to hunting, let out a startled oath, then just as it seemed that nothing could save either of them, he grabbed Andhra roughly and flung her bodily to one side. She fell on her back among the debris of the shattered trees, while he flung himself after her with such violence that he collapsed on top of her, breathing heavily.

They lay rigidly while the creature thundered by. Had it spotted them? Would it return?

Listening intently, they heard it crashing away into the jungle, and slowly relaxed.

"We should be safe now, but it was a close shave," he mumbled.

With danger past, normal reactions returned to Andhra. She was sharply aware of his warm bulk above her, his face, scrubby, insect-bitten, but still strongly male, almost touching her own. Strange, languorous sensations flowed over her, threatening to engulf her in a rising tide of desire.

He laughed softly. "So you do want me, as much as I want you. What point is there in fighting against it? What better place to find paradise than here in this primeval jungle, where nature rules supreme and man-made laws are a myth?"

Sanity returned then like a shower of cold water. "That's not true, John. Any illusion of love I felt for you has vanished these past days. You killed it yourself by revealing your true character."

His mouth became hard and cynical. "Nobody is at his best in the conditions we're experiencing. Things will be different when we're back to sanity, rich and free to travel or do as we please. In the meantime, why wait? I'm crazy for you. If I take you now, you, with your quaint ethical code, will feel bound to marry me, and you won't regret it, I promise."

Such anger as she had never known before now possessed her. To only one man could she freely surrender herself, and if that could never be, she would remain a virgin to the end of her days.

"Get up and let me go!" she said through clenched teeth. "If you so much as touch me I'll shoot you dead. I swear it!"

"You little spitfire! I believe you would too!"

It was hard to say what might have followed, for at that moment Mark's voice was heard calling quite near.

"We're here!" Andhra answered, struggling frantically to free herself from the demanding hold.

Realizing when he was beaten, John rose with a scowl. Andhra struggled to her feet just as Mark and Akbar burst into the clearing.

"Are you all right? What's happened?" Mark asked. "We heard an elephant trumpeting and a shot, and feared you might be in trouble."

"We almost were," Andhra said breathlessly. "The rogue elephant who did this returned, but John acted quickly and now the beast has made off."

"Leaving us plenty fuel," Akbar said.

They each gathered as much as they could manage and carried it down to the boat, then returned to the jungle. This time Mark was lucky enough to shoot a couple of jungle fowl, while the others gathered plantains and mangoes.

A rustling in the undergrowth sent them all diving for

cover. Mark cocked his gun, waiting expectantly, when out stepped a bristly wild pig followed by five piglets. She trotted past, snout to the ground, snuffling for tasty morsels. The piglets followed, the last one too tardily, thereby sealing his doom. Mark's bullet bowled him over and the rest of the family fled with squeals and grunts.

"Roast suckling pig tonight," Akbar said. "Very good."

It was a cheerful party that returned to the boat. Andhra strove to thrust the episode in the jungle behind her, and treated John with cool reserve. From now on she would take care not to be alone with him.

Her resolution was not to be tested. For them all, the ordeal of their flight from Chandipur was drawing to an end. That same evening, the tributary on which they chugged along joined the broader Hooghly River, and now they were only about forty miles from Howrah.

"Howrah stands on the south bank of the river, Calcutta on the north," Mark explained to Andhra and Jenny as they stood watching the now much more animated scene. "The East India Company has offices in both cities, but I think we'll make for Howrah. The railway terminal and station is there, so of course I know the chief of that office best."

Boats of all kinds now plied up and down the water, while the banks were less wild. Little villages clustered thick and fast, and the occasional town dominated by the graceful minaret of its domed mosque. The river, as usual, was the focal point for man and beast. Great ugly water buffaloes wallowed in the shallows, ridding themselves of dust and ticks. Women in rainbow-hued saris washed pots and clothes or filled their shining brass water urns. Men and boys fished, tended boats, or squatted in the sun, leaving the work of the fields to the women.

Andhra and Jenny could have stood at the rail forever, watching the exhilarating scene, but Mark, intercepting the curious stares of the men in boats they passed closely, grew uneasy and urged them under cover of the awning.

"I know you're still wearing saris, but they don't make you

completely convincing as natives. Native women don't stand around on boats enjoying the passing scene. If they're aboard at all, they're either working or sitting decorously out of sight."

"That is so," Akbar declared. "Until we are knowing if this eastern territory has escaped the mutiny, we must take care."

John, perhaps resenting Mark's leadership now that they were almost back to civilization, was all for going first to Calcutta itself.

"With the situation back at Chandipur Fort so critical, won't it save time to make straight for Government House?" he suggested. "Even if we don't see the Governor-General, Lord Canning himself, there'll be others competent to send help quickly."

Mark, thinking of the magnificent new building, the most impressive modern structure in India, shook his head.

"You forget we don't yet know how things stand on the east coast. If the rebellion has spread, that is most likely where it would flare up. The less illustrious office in Howrah is our best bet. I know Richard Stewart, the chief engineer there, quite well. I'm sure to get through to him more quickly and he'll do the rest."

They purposely reached the busy dockside of Howrah at dusk. Several East India Company ships were moored here, both river craft and oceangoing vessels. Here Akbar quietly stole ashore to investigate, returning shortly after with the welcome news that all seemed normal in the town. Though there had been unrest, actual mutiny had not broken out, neither here nor across the broad river in the great city of Calcutta itself.

"Then this is the time to leave this old tub," Mark decided. Under cover of darkness, the bedraggled party of women and children, and equally unkempt men, would provoke less notice than in broad daylight.

They disembarked, carrying the sleeping children, to find the familiar pattern of garbage-strewn narrow streets littered with pitiful bundles of rags that were actually human beings.

Deformed lepers and maimed beggars huddling together outside shuttered shops brought sharply home to Andhra the destitution and misery of India's poor.

It was only a short walk to their destination, the Howrah branch of the East India Company. At this late hour of the day, they found the part of the building fronting the street dark and barred except for a faint light glimmering in an upstairs window.

"It's a bigger place than it appears," Mark said, ringing vigorously on the bell. "It extends a good way at the back, into a compound enclosing Stewart's bungalow, servants' quarters, and other offices."

Tardily, two caretaker-guards opened a small square in the stout door, peering out and demanding to know what business was so urgent that it could not wait until morning.

Mark fished his Company identification card from the pocket of his torn and dirty tunic and passed it through.

"Very urgent business, since it concerns the safety of the fort at Chandipur. The dwindling British there are fighting for their lives, so let me in and conduct me at once to Chief Engineer Richard Stewart."

The guards studied the pass, then with a deferential "Yes, sir" slid back bolts and opened the door.

"This way." They glanced with disapproval at the unkempt party in their unconventional garb, but locked the door behind them and bid them follow as they led the way through a long passage into a compound and finally to an imposing bungalow.

The sitting room into which they were ushered might have been the drawing room of some good-class home in suburban London, with its rich carpet, chintz-covered chairs and chaise longue, well-filled bookcase, and plush tablecloth. All imported at length in Company ships from England, over thousands of miles of ocean. The lady and gentleman who greeted them were equally British upper class in their impeccable attire.

The latter came forward with outstretched hand.

"Mark Copeland, by all that's wonderful! I'm surely glad to see you safe and well. By the smattering of information we could glean, almost the entire center of the country is in rebellion. I pictured the outlying railway project in ruins and you killed. How did you escape this far?"

"It's quite a story, sir. It will keep. The first thing is a bath and rest for these weary women and children. This is Mrs. McQueen, widow of the Chandipur garrison surgeon, killed in action, hoping for a passage home."

"My condolences, ma'am. I fear there will be many such bereavements when all comes to light, and worse. Whole families wiped out. These are indeed black days for the Company, and Britain too. I fear the great trading network we have built up this past century and more will never survive in the form we know."

As he was speaking, his wife had summoned a house boy, who now conducted Margaret and the children to a spare bedroom. Jenny went too, to help with the little ones, but Andhra elected to stay. She was desperate to hear anything that might have filtered through regarding the situation in Chandipur, particularly regarding her father.

But Richard Stewart knew nothing of the way the revolt was going in the smaller garrison towns. Even Delhi had not been recaptured yet, he informed them. A field force had been dispatched under the command of General Barnard, but tragically he had died of cholera during the first week of July.

"We are desperately short of troops in the near vicinity," he said somberly. "We need thousands more to swell the relieving forces. Ceylon, Madras, Rangoon, Singapore, and even England have been urged to help. They are all sending armed forces, but of course travel by sea, although speeded up by steam, is still painfully slow in a situation so urgent. Even when they arrive in Calcutta, it takes about six weeks to get an assault force up-country."

Mark nodded, frowning. "It's tough luck that the railway only runs for a comparatively short way from here. It would have helped enormously had it been connected with the Chandipur venture. Pushing upriver with the water in monsoon flood is hard going, and bullock train even worse."

"How about the Gurkhas of Nepal?" John put in. "A splendid fighting force, and still loyal to the British, I'll stake my oath."

Stewart nodded. "They've been contacted and are on the way south, but again the rains are likely to delay them, with a stretch of jungle to cross."

"But, Mr. Stewart, you can't just leave the smaller garrisons to their fate," Andhra said in dismay. "Chandipur Fort was in a desperate state when we escaped, to try to save the lives of Margaret and her children. Heaven knows how things are going now, especially as cholera had broken out."

Richard Stewart sighed. "I'll have a word with Government House across the river. The Governor-General will send help if he can, I'm sure, but the bitter truth is, we just haven't the loyal troops available. We're outnumbered thousands to one. About three thousand British to forty million Indians."

Margaret and Jenny returned, looking slightly less unkempt, and they all sat down to dinner.

The fish curry, mango tart, and halva, a delicious sweetmeat, were a feast after their recent mode of life, but none of them could really enjoy it in this somber situation.

"The old prophecy seems about to come true," Mark said as they finished the meal with a pot of tea. "That the East India Company would last for only a hundred years after Clive, and then go out like a light."

Stewart nodded. "True enough, but *you'll* have no need to fret, young man. Progress will still go on, under some other rule, no doubt, and railways will come high on the list in a land of such vast distances. There was talk of them expanding in all directions before this trouble began, as you'll know well enough."

"I do indeed."

He glanced at Jenny with a fond smile. She smiled back, full of confidence in her man. He would always carve his way out of any difficulty and come out on top.

Andhra fought down the bitter pang that went through her. Out in the compound someone played soulfully on a sitar and sang an accompaniment to his lost love. It reminded her poignantly of Prince Ranjana and her own brief romance, ended almost before it had begun. All she had left was the golden amulet. It had brought her through many dangers to the safety of the coast, but she wished passionately that he had kept it in the face of his own danger.

"When do you think I'll be able to set sail for England?" Margaret asked at the close of the meal.

"Fairly soon, I should say," Richard Stewart answered. "We're expecting a large oceangoing steamer in about a week's time, with a contingent of Madras forces. Unless it's urgently needed to bring in more reinforcements, the Governor-General may decide to send it off to England packed with severely wounded men and bereaved women and children. They are trickling into Calcutta daily, and we can't guarantee that trouble won't break out here, so the sooner we can get a shipment off, the better."

With three young children, the prospect of a two and a half months' voyage via the Peninsular and Orient route, with possibly a sixty-hour overland journey by horse-drawn stagecoach across Egypt to Alexandria, was anything but pleasant. Yet Margaret felt happier than she had done for weeks at the thought of leaving this vast, fateful land behind.

Jenny, of course, would be remaining in India with Mark. Nothing would part them now, that much was clear. And she herself, Andhra reflected. What did fate hold in store for her?

It all depended on what was happening in Chandipur, and how Father would come through the siege, if indeed he came through at all. On this somber speculation, Andhra presently went up to bed with Jenny. Tonight she would sleep in physical comfort, but mentally there was little to bring her joy or satisfaction.

CHAPTER 14

The days dragged by, with little to divert them from their anxious speculation about what was happening in Chandipur. Richard Stewart decreed that it was safer for the women and children to remain within the compound, for although Calcutta and Howrah were not in open revolt, there was an undercurrent of unrest among the sepoys there which could flare up at any time.

Then one evening as darkness was closing in and Andhra had resigned herself to another night of waiting for news, there was an impatient tattoo on the knocker of the street door. A minute later, the house boy burst in, full of excitement.

"A small party of refugees. They are asking for you. They are coming from Chandipur. One is badly wounded. He says he is Major Hilton."

Andhra and Jenny cried out together, then dashed out into the lobby, beside themselves with both joy and apprehension.

Half a dozen weary wounded British soldiers, in torn, filthy tunics, confronted them. Two hung between crutches, one had his arm in a sling, another could scarcely see for head bandages. The sixth, and most important to the two girls, lay in a litter, unable to walk at all.

"Oh, Father, thank God you're safe, but so pale and gaunt, and terribly wounded," Andhra said chokingly.

"How did you escape, and what of the others in Chandipur Fort?" Richard Stewart asked as he appeared with Mark and John.

"There are no others," Major Hilton said in a tired voice. "All wiped out by rebels or cholera. So should we be, but for a stroke of luck. I'll tell you about it over a drink, if you'd be so good as to give us something, Stewart."

"Of course, my dear chap!" He dispatched the house boy and soon, installed in the sitting room over a whiskey and soda, the men were talking of their long-drawn-out ordeal, when numbers dwindled daily, winnowed out by disease or the bullets of rebels.

"It seemed the end, when only half a dozen of us were left," Major Hilton said, "and all of us wounded. We'd vowed never to surrender, but we knew that we could hold out no longer and would surely be overwhelmed the following day. Then that night a miracle happened."

They all looked expectantly at him.

"Prince Ranjana, driven from the palace at the beginning of the mutiny because he and his family had befriended the British, returned with a few loyal supporters under cover of darkness to revenge themselves on the traitors and retake the palace. But first, by the providence of God, they were brave enough to creep into the fort to do what they could for us. The Prince was horrified to find every man, woman, and child had perished, except for us few, and your small party who had escaped earlier. He got us out and away while the rebels were sleeping and managed to round up a bullock cart to take us down to the river. There we were hidden on a cargo launch that brought us here."

Andhra could scarcely speak for the wild clamor of her heart, but she must know. She *must*.

"What happened to the Prince?" she managed at last.

"He went on to storm the palace. God knows if he succeeded. I believe a bunch of the rebels were well entrenched there. I hope he did, because I certainly owe my life to him. He's a brave fellow."

Andhra nodded, unable to speak.

As though suddenly aware of her concern, her father looked at her with the dawn of understanding. "Oddly, he was intensely concerned about you. Relieved that you had escaped from the hellhole that the fort had become, but sorry to have missed you. You must have made a terrific impression on him the night you partnered him at the palace."

"Andhra always makes a terrific impression," Jenny cut in, anxious to divert attention and spare her sister embarrassment.

While the weary refugees were helped by servants to wash and change into more respectable attire, Andhra was blessedly left to her own thoughts, chaotic in the extreme. She knew, without any doubt, why Prince Ranjana had wormed his way into the fort even before carrying out the attack on the palace. It proved the hold he had on his followers that he was able to command their support in the venture, when they were thirsting for revenge on the traitorous dogs at the palace. It also proved the depths of his love for her. No man could risk more than his life for a woman, and the knowledge sent a warm flame of emotion coursing through her.

But what had happened to him since? The warmth was followed by a coldness like the winter snows of the Himalayas, as she pictured him with his small band storming his way into the regal home of his birth, fighting for the honor of his family and to avenge the atrocities committed since the mutiny began. Could he possibly emerge victorious, or would it prove only a gallant but tragic end to his young life?

This contingency was so appalling that she refused to contemplate it. And yet, had he been alive and well, surely he would have made his way in disguise to Calcutta. Knowing that she and her party would finally end up on one or the other bank of the Hooghly River, unless the hazards of the flight proved too great. He would never rest until he had sought and found her again.

She must give him time, she reasoned, finding any excuse as to why he had not yet come, except the dreadful possibility that he was dead. Perhaps he had been badly wounded and was lying low somewhere, tended by one of the faithful few who had not succumbed to the urge of plunder and destruction.

But time was running out. At the end of a further week, a hospital ship lay moored on the river, impatient to sail while the port was still free. Places were allocated to the severely wounded and to orphans and widows. Major Hilton, who with his left leg severely shattered and other wounds could never soldier again, was given a cabin, and Andhra naturally expected to accompany him and help take care of him on the long voyage home. Margaret and her children were also accommodated.

John was drafted to a company of Gurkhas from Nepal, being sent up-country to try to break the siege of Lucknow, after the failure of General Havelock's attempt. He seemed singularly unconcerned when he bid Andhra goodbye, and she suspected that he would soon find some way of leaving the Army and India for good.

Jenny, of course, refused to be parted from Mark, so a quiet ceremony that made them man and wife was performed at Government House. Mrs. Stewart lent her a pale blue muslin dress, in which she looked quite pretty, and afterward laid on a small celebration breakfast. Her sister was so blissfully happy that Andhra rejoiced wholeheartedly for her, but afterward, when the newly married couple had left for a short break in an untroubled spot further down the coast, the reaction came. She spent a sleepless night raging against the fate that decreed she must leave India without knowing what had become of Ranjana, or if she would ever see him again.

Yet once they had left India behind, she found plenty to banish introspection. Unstintingly she did all she could to make her father's painful lot more bearable. Apart from his physical discomfort, there was the wrench of having to give up his army career before he had reached retirement age. Fortunately, he would be granted an adequate pension by the Company when he reached England, so would not have additional financial worries.

Nor would any problem arise as to where they would live. Aunt Emma's house, which of course now belonged to them, would be waiting in sedate Prittlewell to welcome them as it had done in school days. Rambling and stuffed with old-fashioned furniture, it still had a certain charm and would prove a welcome refuge to the two shattered casualties of the Indian mutiny.

Margaret, too, would have no problems when she reached England. She would be met by her parents and taken straight to their home, where they would no doubt take great pleasure in coddling their daughter and spoiling the children.

Andhra was glad of her company during the tedious voyage, and promised to keep in touch when the ship at last tied up at the East India Docks, in London. Here, Andhra had to say a temporary goodbye to her father. Along with several other severely wounded men he was whisked off to hospital to be patched up, while she was met by Mr. Jordan, their old solicitor, and escorted by carriage to Prittlewell House.

"I'm afraid you are going to feel rather lonely until your father is able to join you, my dear," he said, "but at least you will have a morning woman to do your chores. Mrs. Bennet is of excellent character. I engaged her last week, and she now has the house clean and neat, and no doubt there will be a meal waiting when you arrive."

There was indeed a good old English lunch of boiled beef and vegetables waiting, a welcome change from Indian dishes. Mr. Jordan stayed to have it with her, and they both did ample justice to it on this chilly late-autumn day.

"I'd forgotten how cold England was," Andhra said with a grimace, stirring up the log fire in the dog grate when the meal was finished. "I must buy some new winter clothes."

"Of course, my dear. There is a substantial sum at your disposal, left by your aunt. I'll advance you as much as you need until your father's pension comes through. You'll have no worries on that score."

He left soon after, emphasizing that she could contact him at his office anytime she needed help or advice. After Mrs. Bennet had cleared and washed up, she left too, and suddenly Andhra found herself quite alone for the first time in her life.

It would have been easy to wallow in self-pity, but she was made of sterner stuff. Calmly, she reviewed the days ahead and what she could most profitably fill them with.

There was Father to be visited in hospital twice a week. With a long carriage drive each way, that would fully occupy two days. The rest must be filled with shopping, taking care of the house, and generally keeping the flag flying until such time as Father could join her. Though Mrs. Bennet would do the rougher chores each morning, it would still leave lots of dusting and lighter tasks, as well as preparing her own supper.

She glanced into the crowded drawing room, with its fussy whatnot filled with ornamented china, its crammed mantelpiece, and the many photographs standing around. Enough work here to keep her busy for hours, but how dull. She would pack most of it carefully away in boxes and stow them in the attic, where she and Jenny had delighted to rummage during school holidays.

Thinking of Jenny brought swift nostalgia. How strange that her shy, mousy little sister was now a contented wife, serenely facing a life of adventure with pioneering Mark, while she herself, cool, determined, and outshining Jenny in every way, was now committed to the life of a suburban spinster, caring for a sick father and renouncing all thought of love and marriage. And Jenny, an English girl, was destined to live in India, while she herself, Indian-born, was banished to England by Father's disability.

It would have been easy then to break down and wallow in the depths. Instead, she donned bonnet and cloak and went for a brisk walk to Priory Park, a favorite spot of hers in the old days.

There were still autumn flowers to be enjoyed, and the tints of autumn leaves, as well as the old priory museum. She lingered there until closing time, then hurried back through the dusk to the too silent house.

So began the pattern of her days. With courage and hope at first, confident that it would not be long before her father was able to join her. But his injuries were more serious than she had realized. He needed not one but several operations on his shattered leg, and a chest wound, too long neglected on the voyage home, was causing trouble.

Day succeeded humdrum day. Weeks stretched into months. Christmas came and went, bleak and lonely. Jenny's long chatty letter from India only served to emphasize her own plight.

She and Mark were now settled in the delightful hill station of Darjeeling, Jenny wrote, with a glorious view of the mountains and one of the highest peaks in the Himalayas. The scenery was magnificent, everywhere so fresh and green after the parched plains, and terraced tea plantations cascading down the hillsides, from which came the renowned Darjeeling blend.

"You'll be glad to know that regarding the mutiny the British are now regaining the upper hand, with nearly all the strategic cities and garrisons freed. Mark says it is only a question of time before everything is back to normal. All except the East India Company, unfortunately. That is finished forever. The British Crown will take over, and Victoria be declared Empress of India, it is said.

"It will mean a further expansion of the railways, Mark says. He is doing a preliminary survey to see if a track up to Darjeeling will be possible. It will be a winding, difficult layout, but so useful for the tea trade and the many officials and their families who flock here from Calcutta to escape the heat and the rainy season. If the plan goes through, it will mean many years' work for Mark, and we'll be able to stay in this heavenly spot. You and Father must come out for a long visit as soon as he is well enough. You'll both love it.

"We are sorry to hear that Father's wounds are causing such a protracted stay in hospital, and hope he will soon be home with you. It must be a lonely and anxious life you are leading just now, poor Andhra, while I'm so happy and loved. Mark is the most devoted husband."

No mention of Prince Ranjana. That was the most galling part of all. Had he been alive and well, Andhra felt certain, he would have got in touch with Government House in Calcutta regarding her whereabouts, who in turn would have referred him to Jenny and Mark in Darjeeling. Knowing how she felt toward the Prince, Jenny would certainly have mentioned it had she heard the smallest detail about him.

So it looked as though her ill-starred dream of love was well and truly over.

There was nothing to do but grit her teeth and struggle on.

Winter gave way to spring, and now the question was not when Father would be able to leave hospital and join her, but if he would ever leave at all. His lungs were now giving trouble in the aftermath of the chest wound and the outlook was not good.

Andhra had to face the fact that soon she could find herself quite alone, with Jenny, her only relative, a long voyage away. What should she do in those circumstances?

The thought of lingering on here, aimlessly living out a useless life with only a cat for company, was anathema to one of Andhra's spirit. After that devastating interlude in India, daily facing danger or death, any such prospect was impossible.

Jenny's offer, made with the best intentions, was equally impossible. "If anything happens to Father," she had written, "you must sell up, come out here and make your home with us. You and I have always been congenial to one another, and Mark is so tolerant that he would make no objection. It would be much better for you than being alone."

For a meek, milk-and-water miss perhaps, Andhra reflected. To one of her own pioneering spirit, it smacked too much of the poor relation intruding on the privacy of a happily married couple. It would never work for long.

But as a first foothold in returning to India, it would be useful. Once entrenched there, with a reasonable income of her own, she could soon become independent. In that vast, poverty-stricken land, there was endless work crying out to be done. Clinics and schools to be founded, missionary work of educating and nursing the poor and needy. Obstacles to face and overcome. Challenges to be met and conquered.

India was her native land, no matter how short a time she had actually lived there. It called irresistibly to her to come home, and that she would do one day.

This was what she wanted, she realized dispassionately, if marriage to the one man she had ever really loved was denied her.

So her future was decided upon in her own mind when, on a

late spring day, she returned to Prittlewell House alone after her father's funeral to sort out any remaining personal effects of Aunt Emma's.

The weather was as somber as the ceremony she had just left. To stop herself from brooding, she must keep busy, she decided over a cup of tea. Mr. Jordan would handle everything in his own efficient way. The sale of house and contents, the booking of a passage to India for her.

"Take the first one available," she had instructed him. "There's nothing to keep me here now."

As it could be only a matter of days, she would begin packing at once, she decided, reflecting with satisfaction on the stock of muslin gowns and other tropical clothes she had bought for this expected outcome.

After the refreshing tea, she mounted the two flights of stairs to the attic, to drag out the trunk she recalled seeing there. A sturdy affair, leather-bound and with brass padlocks, it would hold all she cared to take.

As it was heavier than she had realized, she left it on the landing until the following morning, when Mrs. Bennet would be there to help her down with it, and turned her attention to the rest of the things.

Mostly junk or unwanted items, stowed away up here over the years and forgotten. The only attractive piece was a small rosewood desk used by Aunt Emma in her youth and discarded when she had adopted the more imposing desk in the study on her father's death.

Oddly, she had been left in exactly the same situation in which she, Andhra, now found herself today, the latter realized. A dutiful daughter left high and dry on a parent's passing. But whereas Emma had lingered on, a confirmed old maid, her only highlight the care of young Andhra and Jenny during the school holidays, Andhra had no intention of emulating her. Her thirst for adventure was too great.

The desk was locked, as it had always been when she and Jenny had played around up here. Now she had the power to open it.

She took the bunch of keys from her pocket and tried them

until she found one to fit. Then with a stir of anticipation she opened the lid.

There, neatly stowed, were the relics of a young girl's hopes and dreams. Scented programs of ghostly balls, fading artificial flowers, a diary bound in blue leather, a string of single pearls, and, most poignant of all, a lock of curly black hair wrapped in tissue paper and labeled "Dear David's Hair."

Who was David? Andhra tried to recall the little she had heard of Aunt Emma's past.

Her father had been a captain on one of the East Indiamen in the old sailing days. On voyages which lasted many months, it was the custom for wives to be taken along. His own wife being dead, he had taken his daughter instead, perhaps considering that she would be safer under his eye than left to her own devices.

David, Andhra learned from the diary when she glanced through it, was a handsome young midshipman under training. He and Emma had fallen deeply in love and vowed to marry one day, but that was not to be. He, Emma's father, and several deckhands had been washed overboard and drowned while weathering a typhoon when plowing through the Bay of Bengal to Calcutta. It must have been a frightful time for young Emma, losing them both together, Andhra thought with a pang.

There had been happier times before that, parties and balls at various residencies while the ship was in port at Bombay, Madras, and Calcutta. But Emma's carefree youth had been short. After the tragedy she had retreated to this family home and lived out her numerous remaining years a confirmed spinster. What a waste, Andhra reflected. She herself must avoid that at any cost.

Slowly turning the pages, Andhra found scraps of Emma's life coming vividly alive.

"February 10, 1816. A most agreeable evening at the ball given by the company in the residency at Madras. Dear David contrived the supper dance with me, and several others, in spite of the disapproving glances of a stout matron with two plain daughters, and a singular lack of partners."

"March 3. Today I attended a splendid durbar given by the Governor-General at the residency in Caclutta. We were entertained by fighting elephants, which I found rather alarming, and native music, which is monotonous yet pleasant. David and I managed to slip away and wander through the gardens. We exchanged locks of hair and vowed true love through Eternity."

Andhra's smile was tender as she turned the page. Emma had kept her vow, and hopefully now wandered forever in celestial gardens with her lost love.

"March 21. Exceedingly hot. Drove in a carriage with Mrs. Maybury along the waterfront to try and catch a breeze. We were held up by an overturned bullock cart, and an Indian fortune-teller begged for rupees to tell our fortunes. I was for holding back, but Mrs. Maybury laughed and gave him some coins, saying these men were uncannily farsighted. The old native told her pleasing news, but mine was not so good. I would never gain my heart's desire, he said, but would live alone in a cold land. Yet someone connected with me would one day return to India and find true happiness and lasting love. I felt quite cast down all day."

With fast-beating heart Andhra closed the book. Surely the someone connected could only mean herself. Was she destined to meet Prince Ranjana again? If only she could see into the future like the old fortune-teller. But it would not be long before his prophecy could be put to the test, and, oh, how she prayed that it would come true.

Then doubts returned. Surely that someone meant Jenny. It was foolish to encourage any hope of ever meeting Prince Ranjana again after this long silence. She was merely deluding herself and adding to her unhappiness.

CHAPTER 15

How glad Andhra was to sight Bombay.

They would remain in port for several days, the captain informed the passengers, to off-load goods and pick up more passengers and goods for Madras and Calcutta. Anyone who wished might go ashore, but ladies should not go unescorted in a strange and foreign port.

"It is certainly not strange to me," Andhra's cabin mate declared. "I know the city well enough, and nothing would prevent me visiting the nearby mission school, with or without an escort. You, of course, are in a different category. So young and inexperienced. It would be most inadvisable for *you* to set foot ashore alone, my dear Andhra, but you are welcome to come with me if you wish."

There was nothing Andhra would have liked better than to see the mission school, but not in Gertrude Harrington's company. Several weeks of close confinement with her had sorely tried Andhra's patience. The captain had meant well enough when he berthed them together at the start of the voyage, believing that he was doing Miss Andhra a favor in giving her the protection of a middle-aged lady missionary. Miss Harrington meant well, no doubt, but she was so straitlaced, so given to lecturing and ordering others around, as if they were ignorant natives, that Andhra welcomed a few hours' respite from her.

So she hastily declined on the plea of a headache.

"Well, perhaps tomorrow," Miss Harrington called as she strode to the gangway, and so out of sight, a formidable figure in her voluminous skirt and large hat tied on by a veil.

Andhra had diversion in plenty sitting on deck watching the animated scene all around as thin, wiry coolies heaved packages about, on and off the various ships. Chests of tea, bales of cotton, pepper, and spices. Hot and tiring work in such a humid climate, but of course they were used to it.

Occasionally a passenger came aboard, followed by a sweating coolie humping his trunk. Andhra scarcely glanced at these, being more interested in the general scene, a welcome change after weeks of nothing but their own ship. Until presently a voice that she would have known in a thousand fell on her ears. A mere phrase of Urdu as the new passenger paid and dismissed his bearer, it struck an immediate chord and thrilled her to the core.

"Prince Ranjana," she whispered incredulously, scarcely able to form the words for emotion.

As though the murmur had reached and called him, he strode up to where she sat in seclusion and stopped dead, as amazed as she.

"At last we meet again," he murmured at length, in a low, intense voice. "How often I have thought of you, longed for you, wondered how you fared and where you were through these past months."

"I, too," she said as he took the faded canvas chair next to hers. "I feared you must have been killed when you stormed the palace after freeing my father from the fort. That was brave of you, and so typical, but why did you never contact me again? I waited so hopefully in Howrah until forced to sail for England with the wounded and refugees. How I suffered, concluding that you must have perished in the fray. How could you be so cruel?"

"Not cruel, my dear love, but utterly incapacitated by wounds. The attempt on the palace failed, and I would surely have perished but for my two faithful remaining followers. They whisked me away from danger and eventually got me to a small hospital run by English missionaries. They took me in, tended my head wound and others, and nursed me back to health. At first I had quite lost my memory, but with growing strength and healing of the wound it gradually returned. When I recalled you, I was almost beside myself with anxiety, wondering what had become of you. By the time I was able to contact the East India Company in Howrah, they said you had long sailed for England with your father, while your sister was married and living in Darjeeling."

Andhra nodded. "Father never recovered from his wounds. He died over two months ago, and India called me back. I'm bound for Calcutta and then up to Darjeeling to join Jenny until I decide what to do."

He laughed softly.

"That is already decided, my dear lost love."

She colored.

"Jenny never mentioned you in her last letter, so I suppose your contact was quite recent, that is, if you managed to contact her at all."

"Quite recent. The Company contacted them for me. They are well and happy and assured me they would be very glad to see me if I cared to make the journey. It is not an easy one up to Darjeeling, but nothing would have deterred me, especially as they said you would no doubt be joining them soon."

"Kismet," Andhra murmured. "Both of us bound for the same destination, and meeting on the very same ship. It had to be."

"It had to be," he echoed.

Now, with such an escort, going ashore was simple. They paced slowly along, scarcely taking in anything of the passing scene, conscious only that they were together at last, the mutiny over, and life again a thrilling adventure before them.

"Now that the East India Company is virtually finished, and the British Crown taking over, there are changes ahead," Andhra said. "However, Mark and Jenny don't seem to mind. There's talk of a big expansion of railways, including a line from Siliguri to Darjeeling, so they are confident of Mark's future. But now, what of you, Ranjana? With the palace looted and destroyed, your family must have lost a great deal, if not all."

His expression became somber. "That is true, but being the younger son, it does not directly concern me. My brother will try to restore the palace for himself and his sons, but I feel it is now time for me to strike out on my own. My late uncle had no son of his own, so has left me his estate. With loving care it can be made beautiful. I intend to take up residence there and do as much as I can for my people and country. Progress is vital for India. Railways, schools, hospitals; all are urgently needed. The British have shown us the way. We must carry on. You will marry me, daughter of heaven, and reign with me as my princess, helping me with your love and courage to great achievements. How beautiful you will look dressed in your natural costume, a sari of shimmering silk. Tell me you will come."

Her eyes said it all. Nothing would give her greater delight. To be with her prince forever, aiding his work, bearing his sons. What more could any Indian maiden ask?

"We'll be married in Darjeeling. Jenny will be so pleased for us both, and she is all the family I have now."

"But not for long, my pearl of great price."

"Why do you sigh, my prince?"

"Only because Darjeeling is so far off, and you are so near, dear one. You will not understand, but one day you will."

"I understand perfectly." She touched the outline of the amulet that had hung beneath her dress through all the vicissitudes that had befallen her since he had pressed it upon her, and remembered how many times she had pretended that it was his hand caressing her.

"What shall we do tomorrow?" he said. "Something special so that we shall always remember this magical reunion in Bombay."

"I believe there are some marvelous rock carvings on an island near here," Andhra said. "Is it possible to go, do you think?"

"The Elephanta Caves, you mean. What a splendid idea. The island is across the harbor, a pleasant sail away. We can take a picnic there tomorrow."

They smiled in anticipation, before a threatening cloud drove them back to the ship, and the monsoon rain caught them.

The following morning was cloudless, to their great joy.

Andhra cajoled a picnic basket from the galley and they sauntered down to the jetty from where boats plied to and from Elephanta Island, a popular outing for escapees from the heat of the city.

The crossing of about two hours was full of interest. Arab dhows, bringing merchandise from across the Arabian Sea, flaunted their graceful sails, mingling with local fishing boats and foreign shipping. A welcome breeze fanned them, lessening the heat, and glimpses of other islands could be seen.

As they landed on Elephanta, the humid heat enveloped them again. Fortunately the island was well wooded. There were delightful shady walks and sudden glimpses of open sea. They slowly climbed to the highest point and from there had an uninterrupted view of the whole city of Bombay. How beautiful it looked, floating on the shimmering bay.

The sea air had given them both an appetite, so they found a shady spot and enjoyed their picnic.

"Now for the caves," Ranjana said, taking a small oil lamp from the basket. "Without this we should not see the carvings properly, as they are quite dim in places."

"You've been here before, then?" she asked as they set off.

"Once, on a school excursion. I was too immature to appreciate the carvings then. Now, seeing them with you, they will take on a new significance."

At the entrance to the main cave, with its wide columns flanked by sculptured elephants, family groups in colorful saris strolled in and out, most of them equipped with small oil lamps. Ranjana kindled his lamp and they passed inside to the main hall, like a great cathedral with its supporting columns.

"The carvings were done centuries ago by Hindus," he explained. "They are a tribute to Hindu gods and mythology, but more especially to Siva and his many manifestations. There he is."

Siva the great one, who had brought them both safely through many dangers and together at last, Andhra reflected, touching the amulet beneath her dress.

His expression, when she looked at the huge image, was so

benign and understanding that Andhra caught her breath. He seemed to be looking at and through her, knowing all, sanctioning all, casting his blessing on them both.

They passed on to other manifestations of him. Siva the destroyer, crushing evil beneath his feet, and Vishnu the preserver, Siva joyfully dancing, and Siva with his consort, Parvati, being showered with flowers from their followers.

Other caves opening off held equally manificent images. Nandi the bull stood garlanded with orange flowers, while Siva commanded the Ganges to flow down and nourish the parched plain.

They lingered a long time, the small lamp proving invaluable. When at last they emerged into daylight it was to find the groups all gone and the sky threatening another downpour.

"We'd better hurry down to the boats," Andhra said, "but first we must pick up the picnic basket we left on the hill."

It proved costly. The rain began to fall briskly as they reached it, and by the time they had sprinted back to the caves it was falling heavily.

"We'll be drenched before we get down all those steps and across the causeway to the boat landing," Andhra gasped. "We'd better take cover in the cave until it clears."

How large and echoing the cave seemed with just the two of them. Alone with the ancient gods, they might have been centuries back in time.

"Why are you staring so intently at Siva?" she asked, touching his hand, as though jealous of his attention straying from herself.

"I am conveying my thanks, dear one, and asking a blessing on our union. He has brought us through many dangers and safely to each other at last."

She smiled. "I, too, owe him much, and must show my thanks with the greatest offering I can give him. With you beside me, I'll never need its protection again."

Unbuttoning her blouse, she removed the amulet from round her neck and laid it at the feet of the image, among the orange flowers and other offerings that were piled there.

"Now we have his blessing to begin a completely new life together," he said as she came and stood before him.

In the dim light she looked as beautiful and unearthly as Parvati, with her tender mouth and the glimpse of golden bosom in the opening of her blouse. With passionate intensity, he drew her close and kissed each swelling curve again and again until she tingled and burned for him and could not let him go.

"By all the gods ever created, I wish this were our wedding hour," he murmured hoarsely. "Why must we wait for Darjeeling? It is so far off."

"Too far." They must first round the point of Cape Comorin and sail up through the Bay of Bengal. The bay of typhoons, where Aunt Emma's ship had been battered and her true love drowned. How could they take such a risk? Surely now was the hour to surrender herself, here in this hallowed abode of the gods.

"We've waited too long, my prince." Her voice was as passionately urgent as his. "The ceremony can come later, but here and now shall be the consummation of our hearts' desire."

So under the benign smile of Siva, in the mysterious primeval dusk, they found their earthly paradise, and nothing that could come after would ever be as devastatingly wonderful as that secret hour that made them one.